ALL OR NONE

Wall Street Royals, Book 3

TARA SUE ME

WHAT READERS ARE SAYING ABOUT THE WALL STREET ROYALS

"Tara has....delivered a delicious, hot, intense and all-consuming plot, with characters you can't help but fall in love with."

— THE SASSY NERD BLOG

"...sweet and sinful all wrapped up in one."

— KRYSTAL AMORA BOOK REVIEWS

"Tara Sue Me knows how to write erotica and bring you right into that world. But, she also knows how to spin the story around it. It's not all sex ..."

— GUILTY PLEASURES BOOK REVIEWS

"Wonderfully written unexpected and playful."

— KATIE

Copyright © 2021 by Tara Sue Me

All rights reserved.

No part of this book may be reproduced in any form or by any electronic or mechanical means, including information storage and retrieval systems, without written permission from the author, except for the use of brief quotations in a book review.

ISBN ebook: 9781950017249

ISBN print: 9781950017256

THEN
TY

Ty groaned at the pounding in his head and rolled over, promising to get the name of whatever the hell he'd to drink the night before so he could make sure he never touched it again. He should get up and take something for his headache, but the thought of sitting upright made him feel sick. Instead, he forced himself to take deep breaths until the feeling went away.

According to the clock at the side of the bed, it was just after two in the morning.

Hell, what was in that drink?

His memory was fuzzy. He remembered the cocktail party he'd hosted in the Upper West Side penthouse he shared with his wife, Lillian. Lillian hadn't been at the party. She'd left unexpectedly for the hospital because her mother had fallen down her front porch steps. Ty had suggested postponing everything, but Lillian told him there was no need.

The bed shifted beside him and he wondered when she'd returned home. Why he hadn't heard her? She was more than likely naked, based on her bare shoulders. He had a sudden flashback of the wild spring break trip they went on when they were both sophomores in college.

God, they'd gotten so drunk and then spent the next three days only getting out of bed for the necessities. That was the year they added kink into their relationship. Back then, he'd never let a headache stop him from taking Lillian whenever and however he wanted.

How long had it been since he woke her up and had her suck him off?

His dick twitched as if saying '*too damn long.*'

Hell, how long had it been since they'd done *anything* kinky?

All at once, his head didn't seem to hurt as much.

"Lilli," he called softly, using her submissive name. He leaned over to kiss her shoulder. Something was wrong. She didn't smell right. "Lilli?" He asked again.

The bedroom door opened right as Lillian turned in the bed to face him.

"Ty?" Lillian asked, but it wasn't the woman in his arms.

His heart pounded, and he looked over his shoulder to see his name had been spoken by the Lillian at the door.

What?

He looked down to the woman in bed with him. She wasn't Lillian. She wasn't even close. *Jessica?*

"Your new PA, Ty?" Lillian asked, slamming the door behind her. "Seriously? Couldn't you be a little more original and fuck the mail clerk?"

What the hell was going on?

He sat up. "I don't know what you think happened, but—"

Lillian held her hand up. "Don't even."

"Is this your wife, Ty?" Jessica had dropped the sheet, exposing her perky nipples. "Do you think she'll join us?"

CHAPTER 1
LILLIAN

Now

Lillian had never thought of herself as lacking common sense. In fact, she'd always thought the exact opposite. Which explained her shock upon realizing that people with common sense rarely hung out at BDSM clubs waiting for their ex-husbands to show up.

It had never been her intention to act so out of character. Her friend, Jaci, had called yesterday and told her in an excited whisper that Lillian's ex-husband, Ty, had called with a request to reactivate his membership at The Club where Jaci worked. The Club being the exclusive BDSM club he and Lillian had been members of during their marriage. Lillian's response should have been that Ty could go fuck himself and the plane that brought him back to the States. Lillian hadn't stepped a foot inside The Club since their divorce and had never planned to again. That's what she should have said, but she didn't.

No, instead, she decided to visit again. One last time.

Nothing could happen because she visited the place once more. In two days, she'd be on her way to the Florida Keys for two weeks. Not for a vacation, but because two hurricanes had battered the islands, leaving devastation everywhere. Lillian had volunteered to help, thinking it would help keep her mind off Ty.

She should be at her apartment, packing, rather than standing in the large room separating The Club's check-in room and the play areas. Nothing to do about it now, though. She was already here.

The much-too-white room was filling up with people. Most only walked through because of club rules prohibiting any sort of play in the room, but several members sat chatting on one of the many curved loveseats. She didn't see Ty and decided to grab a drink from the bar tucked away in the far corner. Just as she turned to head in that direction, he appeared.

He'd been in London for over two years, so it'd been at least that long since she'd laid eyes on him. How was it possible he'd grown even more handsome? His dark blond hair held a bit of gray, but it didn't make him look old. Rather, he looked more distinguished. The laugh lines around his mouth spoke of his laid-back demeanor.

After everything they'd been through, his betrayal, the divorce he didn't fight her on, being separated by the Atlantic Ocean, and finding their way back to a cordial relationship, the sight of him should not make her body react the way it did. The visceral yearning threatened to pull her across the room to where he stood. She thought about letting it take her, but then she dropped her eyes to the person who'd entered with him.

A woman.

Short with a headful of unruly curls, her eyes flickered from one thing or person to another in unmasked interest and with a hint of trepidation.

A newbie? What the hell?

Just that quickly, she remembered opening her bedroom door and finding Ty in bed with his recently hired PA. Since their divorce, she had tried to date, but had been unable to build up any interest, much less excitement, about doing so. It went without saying; she hadn't found the first person she wanted to sleep with. Of course, the same couldn't be said of Ty.

Not that she cared. She'd divorced him. He could play and sleep with anyone he wanted. It wasn't her business anymore.

Still, she had to get out of the room before he saw her and, even worse, noticed she was alone.

He called her name the second she turned away, but she continued through the doors leading to the public play space as if she didn't hear. He wouldn't follow because he was much too good of a Dom, and the tiny little thing he brought with him looked scared half to death. No way would he bring her into this area or leave her alone while he followed by himself.

She stopped walking for a minute. Hell, did she think he cared enough to follow her? He brought someone with him for crying out loud. His plan for the night probably involved the newbie sub and a private room.

She snorted, causing several people to look her way, though most went on with whatever it was they were doing before. Except, of course, for one guy who must have decided he enjoyed snorting submissives because he changed course and headed in her direction.

Damn it all to hell.

He was attractive enough, with thick brown hair and blue eyes that sparkled as if he was in on a joke, but after seeing Ty in person, there wasn't a man on the planet who could tempt her at the moment. God, she'd forgotten how devilishly handsome her ex was.

"Hello," the Dom said, coming to a stop right in front of her. Damn, he was even more attractive up close. "I'm Eric. I don't recall ever seeing you here before."

His smile and demeanor were charming, but lost on her. "Lillian. I'm an old member," she told him. "Just haven't been part of the scene lately."

"Any reason?" he asked.

She shrugged, not wanting to explain the entire situation to a stranger. "Yes, but nothing I'd bore you with."

"Why do you think I'd be bored?" He was pushing, as one would expect from a Dom, but she wasn't in the mood for anything he had in mind.

"Trust me," she said. "You would be. But it doesn't matter, because I only came to observe tonight. I have no intentions of playing."

"I can take a hint," he said, with a grin. "It's nice to have met you, Lillian. If you decide you'd like to do more than observe the next time you're here, feel free to find me."

"Thank you, Eric," she said, relieved he didn't attempt changing her mind. He gave her a wink before turning and walking away.

She sighed, watching his tight backside as he made his way across the room. Another time, another place, another lifetime, Eric would have turned her head. For the briefest of seconds, she contemplated calling him back. What would be the harm in blowing off some steam for an hour or two? Or blowing him off?

But she'd never been one to play casually.

"Thank goodness you turned him away."

She knew the voice, knew it at the most intimate of levels. Lillian closed her eyes and let the sound wash over her. Enjoying the way it made her skin tingle and her insides grow warm and needy. Then, as sudden as she'd let it wash over her, she shut it off, and turned to face the owner of the voice.

"Ty." She looked him in the eyes, determined not to give into or show any of the emotions running through her body. Not the jealousy, or the anger, and for sure as hell not the desire being around him unwillingly brought out. "How did you think you'd have stopped me if I'd welcomed his advances?"

"I don't know, but he wouldn't have put his hands on you tonight," Ty said as if the entire thing was up to him. Damn cocky arrogant bastard Dom, he never changed.

"I believe you lost the right to have any say on that matter the day we signed the divorce papers," she told him, almost wanting him to say otherwise.

"That doesn't keep me from thinking it or wanting to stop it."

Anger at his words boiled inside of her. How dare he?

"You have some nerve," she said, hands on her hips. "You stroll in here with some pretty young thing who looks like she might pass out at any minute, and then you think you can dictate who I'm with?"

Screw this. Lillian turned away. Maybe Eric hadn't gone far. If she hurried, she might catch up with him before he found someone else to play with.

"Maggie?" Ty asked, as if Lillian would know who he was talking about, would know her name. "Because if she's who you mean, the short woman with the curly hair, it's not what it looks like."

Lillian snorted. "Like I haven't heard that one before." Though, thankfully, Ty had the decency to look uneasy with his own choice of words.

"Maggie is Isaac's PA, and she's completely into him," Ty said.

Obviously, her ex-husband had forgotten who she'd worked with from the time he went to London until a few weeks ago. She had little doubt she knew Isaac better than anyone after working as his PA for years before the illustrious Maggie. And yes, she'd tell Ty, she knew he went to college with the man, but it wasn't the same. She'd worked at his side, day and night, for almost three years.

"Please," she said. "Isaac has never dated women he works with, especially his assistant. There's no way he'd be with her. Even if he changed his mind on that score, I thought you had enough respect for your friend and business partner not to make a move on his woman."

"You thought right," Ty said. "But they aren't together. Or they weren't until a few minutes ago. The only reason I'm standing here is because Isaac showed up and almost lost his shit, thinking the same thing you did."

She supposed it should have made her feel better they'd shared the same reaction. They always had been more like-minded than she and Ty ever were.

"Sorry for jumping to an inaccurate conclusion," she said.

"No worries," he said, his smile returning. "But I have one question. Why are you here tonight?"

She had never lied to Ty, and she told herself she wouldn't start now, no matter how tempting or easy it would be to do so. "I heard you were stopping by. It never occurred to me you would have someone with you. When I saw the two of you enter the main area, I went a bit crazy in my head."

"What did you think would happen if I showed up alone?"

"You said you had one question, that's two." Not to mention, she didn't want to answer that particular question because, totally against her nature , she hadn't thought that far ahead.

Or more to the point, she had, but couldn't admit the answer to herself, much less confess it to him.

"I'm asking." He stepped closer, moving into her personal space. "Because I'm alone now. Which means whatever you thought might happen, remains possible."

"No," she said, because what she wanted was impossible.

"Tell me." He lifted his hand as if to brush her cheek, but she turned her face.

"Don't." If he touched her, it'd be over, she'd surrender to him.

He'd broken her once. She'd be damned if he'd get the chance to do it twice.

CHAPTER 2
TY

Until Lillian turned her head to avoid his touch, Ty hadn't realized there were pieces of his heart left with the ability to break. He'd hoped that his move to London had given her the time and space she needed. For the last eighteen months, their talks had been friendly. Jovial, even. Though now that he thought about it, they rarely talked about anything other than work.

Had it all been a facade? Or had the sight of him with Maggie, no matter how innocent it was, brought back memories of that night to her?

Hell, he wished something would bring back the memories to him. Over two years later, and he had no recollection of anything occurring after he welcomed guests into what used to be their home.

"Step away from her, right the fuck now, or I'll get security," a rough voice said from behind him. "But only after I kick your ass."

Ty didn't move except to look over his shoulder. The Dominant Lillian rejected moments ago stood there, nostrils flaring, and his expression full of rage.

"What?" Ty asked.

The man took a step closer. "She said no twice, which is one time too many. I suggest you leave now while you still have the ability to walk."

Fucking hell, this was the last thing he needed. Ty took a step back because he could only imagine how his interaction with Lillian appeared to a third party. Shit. Nothing about this meeting was going his way. It only took one glance at the way the Dom glared at him for Ty to realize he needed to diffuse the situation now before it escalated into something it didn't need to.

"I know what you're doing, and I'm grateful to you for stepping in when you suspect something's wrong or that someone is in trouble." Ty held his empty hands out because the guy still appeared seconds away from jumping him. "But it's not...." He couldn't finish with *the way it looks*. Damn it all, how many times had Lillian heard that line from him?

Without replying to anything Ty said, the Dominant looked at Lillian. "Are you okay? Do you want me to contact security?"

For a brief second he saw the possibility cross her mind in the way her eyes flicked up at him. He could almost see the, "it would serve you right" in her eyes. As he expected, though, she didn't go through with it. No matter what, she could never be that vindictive. "I'm fine, Eric," Lillian told him, even managing to give the guy a small smile. "Ty's my ex-husband, and I have no reason to fear him. He'd never ignore anyone's use of no."

Eric remained in place, continuing to give Ty the stink eye. "Knowing he's your ex-husband only gives me more reasons not to trust him, but if you say he's not a threat, I'll take your word."

Had it been any other situation or any other submissive, Ty would have admired the way Eric ensured a submissive's well being. Hell, if he thought about it enough, he'd probably be thankful Lillian had someone looking out for her.

However, the truth was it wasn't another situation or another submissive they were dealing with. It it made him damn near rage with jealousy at the thought of another Dom looking out for Lillian.

"I appreciate you ensuring my safety. Thank you," Lillian said, and the tone of her voice made Ty swing his gaze from Eric to Lillian.

Was she flirting with the man?

It took him a second to realize no, she wasn't. She was speaking to Eric normally, but it'd been so long since Ty had heard that particular tone, it only sounded like flirting.

"No need to thank me," Eric said. "I'll be around if you need me."

"I'm actually going to be leaving now," she said.

"Want me to walk you out?" Eric asked with a bit too much glee, even while renewing his glare at Ty.

She shook her head. "That won't be necessary."

Eric looked her up and down. Subtle, but Ty recognized the action from doing it himself to assess a submissive and their response. Eric still wasn't convinced Ty hadn't hurt Lillian recently, or that she was being truthful in saying she was fine with him. Ty remained still and silent.

"Very well," Eric said, but he didn't seem happy about it. In fact, he stood right where he was and crossed his arms over his chest.

"Later, Ty," Lillian said and walked toward the doors leading directly to the locker rooms.

Ty watched until she left, but he wasn't ready to say goodbye to her just yet. Not even for the night. Since he came with Maggie, there had been no need for him to visit the locker room. His only plan for the night was to give her a tour, and he didn't even have to do that anymore since she'd gone off with Isaac. It would be easy to follow or wait for Lillian to come out.

One look at Eric told Ty it would be in his best interest not to be waiting for Lillian to emerge from the women's locker room. He didn't think it was a good idea to wait for her outside the club, either. There was no doubt Eric would watch and wait in both places for him to do that. And getting involved in a fist fight wasn't on Ty's list of things to accomplish for the evening.

Ty nodded a goodbye at Eric and headed straight toward the club's neutral, no-play room, which allowed him to exit the club without going near the dressing rooms. Before stepping outside, he stopped by the front desk to ensure Maggie was taken care of. Not that he could fathom Isaac ever leaving her, or anyone for that matter, alone in an unknown club, but Ty wouldn't be able to forgive himself if something happened to her. Especially with the truth being it was him and not Isaac who'd brought her tonight.

Though the young man working the front desk didn't know Ty, he knew who Isaac was, and assured Ty that Maggie was being well cared for. Ty thanked him, and walked out of the club feeling more upbeat than he had walked in, though he wasn't sure why. At the end of the night, Maggie wouldn't leave him broken and in two million pieces. The same couldn't be said of Lillian.

Not that it changed his mind on what his next step would be, he realized as he flagged down a cab outside the club. Lillian might think they were finished for the night, but he was nowhere close to being finished.

He gave her address to the taxi's driver and looked out the window to the BDSM club. There were only a few windows on the nondescript building, but the main office on the second floor held one that overlooked the very spot he'd just hailed the cab from. Someone moved from behind the blinds. Eric, if Ty had to guess. Probably delighted to see him leave and congratulating himself on winning.

Joke was on him, because Ty hadn't even started fighting.

. . .

CHAPTER 3
LILLIAN

Lillian stepped out of the club, half expecting to find Ty waiting for her. When he wasn't, she couldn't decide if she was surprised or not. Based on what he said prior to being interrupted by Eric, he'd be waiting for her. Perhaps the interaction with Eric had changed his mind. She hadn't seen Ty in almost three years, but she still knew him. Eric's implication he thought Ty intended to act without her consent more than likely had thrown her ex-husband for a loop.

Ty might be a cheater, but he'd never cross the consent line. He wouldn't even toe it.

But of course, Eric wouldn't know that. He couldn't. She smiled at the thought of how Eric had rushed to her side when he thought she was in trouble. Truth be told, she'd always found a Dom's protective nature to be undeniably hot. If she wasn't heading to Florida in two days, she would have given serious thought to agreeing to spend an hour or so with Eric.

However, not only was she headed to Florida, Ty was back in town and that made things....different. At the moment, she wasn't sure to what extent they were different, but somehow seeing her ex affected her more than the knowledge of his return to the States.

On the way back to her apartment, she debated on whether she should tell Ty about Florida. Part of her thought it was crazy she even asked herself the question. Why should she tell him? He was no longer anything to her other than a heartache and sad reminder of what she once had. Or at least, what she once thought she had.

The other part of her accepted the fact that since they had spoken face-to-face, if she were to take off without a word, he'd worry when he wasn't able to reach her. Not that she should care.

But she did.

The realization of how much she still cared left her a little despondent. It'd been close to three years. How long did it take to get over one's ex-husband? She could be nice to herself and say she needed more time. After all, it had always been her intention to live happily ever after with Ty forever. The possibility of divorce had never crossed her mind. You couldn't expect to get over forever quickly, could you? Surely, it took longer than a handful of years. But she feared she'd never get over him.

If she ran the world, all feelings she had for Ty would have ceased the second she found him with another woman in their bed. Likewise, when approached by a fine looking and protective Dominant such as Eric, she would jump at the chance to spend some time alone with him. Unfortunately, she didn't run the world, and whoever did never bothered asking for her opinion on the matter. Which meant the only things she had waiting for at her when she got home were a lonely apartment and a half packed suitcase.

Except when she entered the lobby of her building, Ty was waiting for her.

SHE BLINKED to make sure he wasn't a figment of her imagination. Maybe thinking about him on the way home had somehow tricked her brain into believing he was there. Like a mirage.

But no. Right there he stood. Waiting.

She hated how happy she was, and willed herself not to let it show.

"No one would let me inside," he said.

"Good," she replied. "Security's one reason I chose this place."

"Will you let me in so we can talk?" he asked.

She crossed her arms. "What could we have left to talk about?"

"Lillian, please," he said.

"Please what?"

"Please, let's not do this here."

"Do what? From where I'm standing, all we're doing is talking."

He sighed. "I'd prefer we talk in private."

She bit her tongue. If she didn't, odds were she'd tell him she didn't give a damn what he preferred, and then give him an alphabetized list of times her preferences weren't considered. Doing that, however, would get them nowhere.

"Talking won't change anything," she finally said. "We've already talked about everything there is to talk about, and I don't feel like a rehash. That's my preference."

He studied her. It almost felt as if he was attempting to determine how serious she was. She leveled her gaze at him in what she hoped conveyed, serious as I've ever been.

It must have worked because he sighed and ran his hand through his hair. "I'll tell you what," he said. "Let me in tonight. Let's have one conversation, and if at the end, you still feel the way about me as you feel now, I'll leave you alone."

She raised an eyebrow, not believing a word out of his mouth. "Right. Sure you will."

"I promise, Lillian."

He whispered her name, and its warmth wrapped around her in a way she'd forgotten. Tears prickled her eyes at how tenderly he spoke. It took all she had not to burst out with the truth. She would still feel the same way about him after their conversation as she did right now. But she held her tongue because he didn't need to know she still loved him. Even after everything. She couldn't tell him how she sometimes rolled over in bed and expected him to be there. How when something happened, and she had to talk to someone, he was the first person who always came to mind.

If he knew... If she slipped and told him, he'd never give up. He'd keep thinking if he tried hard enough, she'd change her mind. But she wouldn't. She couldn't.

She decided in that moment to keep her feelings for Ty buried deep inside where no one went, and he'd never know. Her issues with him were never about her feelings. She loved him. Always had. Always would. But she couldn't trust him. And because of that, there was no way of the two of them would ever reconcile to where they once were.

She tilted her head, trying to determine how serious he was. "I let you in, let you talk, and if I still feel the same, you'll leave and won't bother me again?"

"Yes."

"Come on inside."

CHAPTER 4
TY

Ty's sense of victory lasted as he rode the elevator up to her apartment, watched her unlock the door, and stepped inside behind her. It disappeared the instant she turned around to address him. All it took was one glance at the way she stood to know everything he needed. From how she held her back and shoulders, to the look in her eye. Cold and unmoving. Every last inch.

His stomach plummeted. He'd done that to her. He'd made her that way.

"Nothing I say is going to change matters." He spoke it as a statement because he didn't need her confirmation.

"I'm glad you realized that truth sooner rather than later," she said. "Now you can leave and we'll both have time to do something constructive with our evening."

He didn't want to have time to do anything else. He wanted to talk with her. Hell, as far as he was concerned, they didn't even have to talk. He was thrilled to stand in her presence.

He looked around. The apartment she lived in now wasn't as nice as the one they had shared, but then again, his wasn't either. He'd moved not long after the separation, not able to stand living in the space they'd shared.

As expected, her new place was clean and cozy. Somewhat of an open concept, he could see both the kitchen and the living room from his spot in the entranceway. There was a door he assumed to lead to a bedroom.

"Maybe I can help you do something constructive? Hang pictures? Paint?" he suggested.

"Are you trying to be helpful now?"

"I'm trying to do anything that'll keep me here longer." He saw the unasked question in her eyes. Why? He also saw she refused to ask it. "Because it's been three years since I last saw you, and I'm not ready to lose sight of you just yet. There's something about just looking at you that makes happy."

He hoped his words might soften her or make her smile, but they didn't appear to do either.

"In that case," she replied. "It's probably for the best I removed that decision from you altogether."

Removed that decision? "What does that mean?"

"It means the day after tomorrow, I'm going to Florida for two weeks to help with hurricane recovery."

He wasn't sure he heard correctly. Lillian was going to Florida for two weeks? For hurricane recovery? The day after tomorrow? "What?"

Instead of answering, she walked to a nearby table, took a piece of paper from the top, and passed it to him. It was a printed email from a coordinator for a non-profit relief agency. He made a note of the coordinator's name and phone number before handing it back to Lillian.

"Why?" he asked.

Her expression softened for a second, but before he could say anything, she shook her head and walked into the small kitchen. He wasn't sure if he should follow or not. She hadn't told him not to but, she hadn't motioned for him to come with her, either.

Fuck it. He followed her, determined to find out why she felt the need to go to Florida all of a sudden. He'd read the date on the printed email. This trip wasn't something she'd had planned for months. From what he could gather, it'd existed about three weeks. Coincidentally around the time he'd returned to the States.

She turned to look at him, and the tear-filled eyes meeting his took him aback. He rushed to her.

"Lillian," he said. What he really wanted to do was gather her in his arms and do whatever it took to make her tears disappear forever. However, he knew her well enough to recognize that at the moment, she wouldn't welcome either action. Instead, he placed his hand along her lower back and guided her to the small table she had in the room's corner. He pulled out one of the two chairs and settled her into it. "Mind if I sit down with you?"

"No." She wiped a thumb under each eye and gave an enormous sigh.

He waited for her to talk first. The move to London had afforded him time to think, and he spent a lot of that time thinking about the two of them. In looking back over the course of their marriage, he realized he'd always felt the need to fill the silence. Now he realized that there was nothing wrong with silence. In fact, thanks to his other business partner, Lance, and his fiancé, Celeste, Ty had learned some benefits of silence. Which meant if he had to sit at Lillian's kitchen table all night, waiting for her to speak?

He'd sit back and get comfortable. Whatever it took, he would do. He wanted to know what was happening and why she was leaving for two weeks, but he was going to let her take the lead in the discussion.

But it didn't take all night. It didn't even take three minutes. Apparently, Lillian must have somehow figured out he wouldn't push her to talk.

"You want to know why I decided to go to Florida now?" she asked.

"Yes," he said. "It doesn't strike me as something you'd do."

"I'm going because you're back, and I don't know how to live in the same city with you and not to be with you. Because I know how easy it'd be for me to fall back under your spell. I can't do it again." She closed her eyes and took a deep breath, but he knew she wasn't finished yet.

He waited.

Her eyes opened and when she looked at him, he felt as if she saw beyond the part of him he showed everyone and went straight to the part that had always belonged to her and her alone. After all these years, it could never be claimed by another.

"Even now," she said. "Having you here in my apartment, I feel it."

He didn't have to ask what she meant because he knew all too well what she was talking about. In London, where he thought he'd be able to start again, he never made it past one night with a woman. He always found a reason not to call and ask for a second date, and when it all came down to it, they all shared the same reason. None of the women were Lillian. As a result, he was the perpetual bachelor, stuck in a country he didn't belong to and unable to move on.

How could he move on when the best part of him was across the ocean?

"I know," he told her. "I feel it, too."

Her hands were on top of the table, tempting him to touch one. To bring it up to his lips for a kiss. He couldn't help but wonder if her skin still tasted the same or if it'd changed over the last few years. Under the table, he fisted his hands so he wouldn't give into the temptation to find out for himself.

"It's never going to go away, you know." He couldn't help but to lean closer to her as he spoke, what with it being such a small table and all. "It's always going to be there between us. If the last three years have shown us nothing, they've shown us that. Do you really think a two-week stint in Florida is going to make a difference?"

"Not really." She shrugged. "But at least it'll give me something else to think about for a little while."

He leaned even closer to her, and this time, she shifted more toward him. Whether she knew or not, he wasn't sure. "Do you think about me a lot, Lillian?"

Her lips parted just enough for her tongue to wet them. She wasn't aware she was doing it, or at least, that was what she'd always said in the past whenever he mentioned how it drove him wild. The sight of the pink, wet tip brushing across those soft lips.

Fuck.

"I'd be lying if I said anything different," she finally admitted.

He'd spanked her for lying before. With that thought, an image of her naked, her ass bare and exposed for him flashed before him. He fisted his hands harder. Damn it. This was not the time for his dick to decide to join in and give advice. But between her tongue and the image of her anticipating his discipline, he couldn't blame his dick for trying.

Regardless, the fact of the matter was Lillian was going to Florida for two weeks to help with hurricane repairs as a way to keep from thinking about him. Nothing about that sounded like a good idea, and it wouldn't work, anyway. Because as much as she'd hate to admit it, he bet at night, when all was still and silent, she'd still think of him.

Except, he reminded himself, she'd be in Florida, and he'd be here.

With that thought he realized he needed more than an evening to win her back. He needed a plan, and there wasn't much time to come up with one. He pushed back from the table. Lillian looked up in shock as he stood up.

"I need a rain check for this evening," he said.

"Are you leaving?" she asked. "I thought you wanted to talk?"

"I do, but not like this. Not tonight."

"Whatever," she said, still sitting down. "Just remember I'm out of here in two days."

He surprised himself when he leaned his head down and dropped a kiss on the top of her hair. "Believe me. It'd be impossible to forget that."

CHAPTER 5
LILLIAN

Lillian spent the next two days in a perpetual rush. Before she'd started packing, she'd made a list. Or rather, she made several lists, but only one of them was items for her suitcase. The other lists were things she had to do, like stop her mail and clean out her refrigerator. Maybe the multitude of lists was overkill, but it was the only way she could ensure everything that needed to be done, got done. Heaven alone knew how many lists she'd made while working for Isaac.

The one thing she didn't have to worry about was work. After stepping down from being Isaac's personal assistant, she hadn't looked for another job. She was fortunate. Her pay from working with Isaac had been much more than she needed to live comfortably. After all, the only person she had to take care of was herself. There was also the very hefty settlement Ty gave her after the divorce, but so far she'd refused to touch any of that money.

She didn't want to go forever without a job and had plans to find one.

As soon as she decided what she wanted to do.

Not that she didn't enjoy being a personal assistant, but it wasn't anything she was passionate about. She had never planned to be a PA. But when Ty, along with friends Isaac and Lance, went into business together, she did anything she could to help. As a newlywed, it thrilled Lillian to work at her husband's side. As time went on and the business grew, she just sort of fell into the role of his assistant.

It worked out beautifully, and they had relatively few issues. People warned them they'd soon dislike always being around each other, but they never did. When Isaac's personal assistant quit, Lillian knew a new person wouldn't be able to jump in and take over the way Isaac needed, so she volunteered. Her plan had been that since Ty was much more laid back and easy going, he could train the new PA, while Lillian ensured everything ran smoothly for Mr. Perfection, aka Isaac. Once the new hire was up to speed, and up to the task of working for Isaac, Lillian would transition back to Ty,

Finding the newbie PA in her bed and with her husband blew that plan to bits.

Lillian had been fine working exclusively for Isaac after that. They had been friends for several years and made an excellent team. In many ways, he was like a brother to her. And it helped that Ty left to manage the office overseas. But when Lance decided he wanted to work in London, so he could be near his girlfriend, Lillian knew what would happen next.

There was no need for two of the partners to be in London, and Ty, being Ty, didn't care. As soon as he heard Lance mention the possibility of wanting to be in London, Ty let him know he was willing to switch. Once the decision was made for the moves to occur, Lillian submitted her notice to Isaac. She gave him six weeks, which should have been more than enough time to find and hire her replacement, and for Lillian to work with whoever it was one-on-one.

For some unknown reason, though, Isaac never got around to looking for a new assistant. Lillian wasn't sure if he was living in the land of denial or if he truly thought she was going to change her mind and ask for her job back. Instead of trying to convince him that, yes, she really was quitting, she created a notebook for whoever he ended up hiring. Isaac continued acting like nothing was going to change. She could still picture his expression on her last day in the office when she started packing her things.

Very different from the packing she was doing now, she thought with a glance at the carry-on bag currently crammed to near overflowing with everything she'd need for the next two weeks. Because of the work she'd be doing and because there was a possibility she'd be sent to multiple areas, it was recommended she pack as little as possible.

As she stared into her closet and checked it against her list, it hit her how drastically her wardrobe had changed over the last few years. She'd had to accompany Isaac to several black tie events, and she'd always considered her outfits for those times to be simple and understated. But stuffed in the back of her closet were the work suits and the gowns she'd favored before the divorce. She ran a hand across the pink fabric of one. When was the last time she wore pink? She couldn't remember.

Another suit caught her eye. Periwinkle blue.

When had periwinkle turned into navy?

In the back, a bright streak of red, visible through the gown's clear storage bag, laughed at the idea of being simple and understated.

Her shoes were different as well. Under the Before the Divorce clothes were heels so high they blew her mind, even knowing she'd worn them. Opposed to the boring as hell sensible pumps with square heels she wore now.

Why had she not noticed how much she'd changed? When did she become this dark and drab shadow of her former self?

She had no idea.

As she stood there, one thought made its way to the forefront of her mind. She might not know when the drab started, but sure as hell knew when it ended.

The two weeks in Florida were going to be more than escape from Ty. Even more than an opportunity to help those in need after the hurricane. It would be a time for her to come out of the shadows and to discover where the woman she was went.

The first obstacle would be the flight. She hated flying. The only times she didn't mind it, was when she'd fly with Ty. He knew she didn't like to fly, but unlike everyone else, who always fell into two groups, those who tried to explain how a metal tube filled with people could soar through the sky, or those who chalked her up to being stupid, he simply took her as she was. He accepted her, and didn't try to change her.

EIGHTEEN HOURS, one delayed flight, one missed connection, four massive lines of irritable travelers, and a rental car the size of a turnip later, Lillian didn't care about discovering anything other than a shower and a bed. Preferably in that order, but she wasn't picky.

She pulled up to the address the non-profit had given her as the headquarters for the project and parked. Odd. It looked more like a high end campground than anything else. The information they had given her stated most of the time the volunteers stayed at local hotels. That being the case, maybe the nonprofit had rented the campground.

Instead of getting out of the car, she took the key out of the ignition and slumped back into the driver's seat. Or as far back as she could go without sticking her head out the back window. Renting a car Maimi and driving to the Keys had seemed like such a good idea while standing at the counter at the airport. It was that or wait to see if she could get on standby for a flight leaving in six hours. A flight, the harried airline employee said, was already overbooked.

Considering the drive to her destination would only take three hours, it seemed foolish to wait six for a flight she more than likely wouldn't get on. Walking to the car rental hub, she decided it would probably be a good thing to have her own transportation, anyway. Since it wasn't required and because the flights had worked out so well when she'd booked them, she'd decided not to worry with a rental.

The only rental available now, unfortunately, was a car so small she worried her carry-on wouldn't fit, and that even if it did, she wouldn't. Against all odds, they both made it inside and Lillian was off to the Keys.

"Thank about what great gas milage you're going to get with this car," the rental car employee said, as he lifted the gate to let her out of the lot.

She said nothing because, honestly, she couldn't believe the tiny little thing even had a gas tank. After a few miles, Lillian found she drove better if she didn't think about how much bigger everyone was, comparatively speaking. Living and working where she did, driving wasn't something she did frequently, and though Miami wasn't Manhattan, it wasn't the backwoods, either.

Mile by frazzled mile, she made her way South. And in less time than she'd expected, because as it turned out she had somewhat of a lead foot, she arrived.

Her eyelids were the only things that felt like lead at the moment. Driving tired wasn't her best decision ever, but the thought of how easily another car would squash her if they were in an accident was enough to keep her wide awake and focused.

Just a little more, she told herself. Check in and find out where she'd be sleeping for the next few days, and then she could get a shower and find a bed. Or find a bed and then shower.

She reached to the side to get her bag when a knock on the window by her head made her yelp.

"Sorry to frighten you," an older gentleman said. "I saw you pull up, but you didn't get out, and I just wanted to make sure you were okay."

"I'm fine, thanks," she said. "Just a bit tired."

He took a step back and helped her out of the car, taking her bag over her protests. "You can get it back inside, but where I'm from, a man doesn't let a woman carry her luggage. Not if he's got two working hands. My name's Tom, by the way. Thomas actually, but they call me Tom."

"Pleasure to meet you, Tom," Lillian said with a grin. Tom looked to be in his eighties, but she wasn't sure. He was on the thin side and had a headful of white hair.

"You must be Ms. Bancroft," Tom said.

"Yes, I am."

"I figured. You're the only one checking in today."

"Really?" She thought there would be more than just her. Looking around, she realized how empty everything looked. "Is there anyone else here?"

"Oh, sure," he said. "Right now, everyone's off working. Where they're at now is about fifteen miles from here. They'll all be back in about two hours."

Two hours wasn't very long. Tom must have noticed her quizzical expression because he continued. "They're finishing up a project today. Once everyone's back, they'll meet and discuss the one they're going to start tomorrow."

They chatted a bit as they made their way toward a large cabin with an OFFICE sign. The air felt thick and damp around her, and she regretted the jeans she'd put on. The weather made them feel as if they weighted twenty pounds.

Tom noticed, but said nothing about it, instead pointing out where the meals were severed and meetings held. Lillian nodded, tying to remember everything, and not think about how hot she was.

"How long have you worked with Restoration?" Lillian asked.

He chuckled. "I don't work for them."

"You don't?" She couldn't help ask. Before she could ask her next question, what was he doing on the property, he answered.

"Not officially, anyway. Not since I busted my knee a few years back, but I hang out and help around when I can. When they're down this way."

"I'm sure they appreciate the help."

"Wouldn't matter if they didn't, they don't have a choice," Tom explained with a laugh. "I own this whole joint."

It wasn't the reply she'd expected at all.

"It's an old resort I bought back in my younger days," Tom continued. "Never did anything with it. Finally decided the world didn't need another useless resort, so I made the decision to let non-profits, church groups, and the like use it when they wanted. With the recent hurricane damage, everyone cancelled. Works out nice for you guys."

Lillian was too shocked to say anything, because, really, who could just buy a resort and do nothing with it? They walked over to an old desk. A two-way radio, a cell phone, and a computer were on top, but instead of reaching for one of them, Tom took a worn business register beside the computer. At Lillian's raised eyebrow, he grinned.

"'I'm not much for computers," he explained and wrote something down.

She waited.

"Come on with me." Tom moved out from behind the deck and beckoned for her to follow him back outside with a wave of his hand.

She took the key he held out. "Thanks."

"The cabins aren't very big and the air conditioning is hit-or-miss on a good day, but they all have a private bathroom and a fan," Tom explained.

They went out the rear door of the office/cabin. The short walk to the outside didn't offer her much of a glimpse into what her accommodations would look like.

The humidity was so intense, Lillian almost wondered if it'd be easier to drink the air instead of breathing. Behind the office was a long line of six identical cabins. Off to the left side was the building Tom mentioned earlier was for meals and meetings.

"Your cabin is right this way," Tom said. "I gave your husband an information packet when he arrived, but be sure to let me know if you have any questions after you look over it."

Lillian stopped in her tracks. "What was that?"

"What part?"

"The part about my husband."

"Ty Bancroft. He arrived late last night."

CHAPTER 6
TY

Showing up at the headquarters for the Restoration project currently underway in Florida the night before Lillian arrived seemed like a great idea right up until the moment she opened the door to the cabin. He expected she'd be pissed, but when he looked up and saw her standing in the entrance way, he saw how wrong he'd been. She was beyond pissed. She was mad as fuck. The door slammed shut behind her.

"You're late," he said with a smile, trying to lighten the mood. "I expected you hours ago."

"What the hell are you doing in my cabin?" she asked.

"It hit me how little I've given back to my community in the last few years. You'd mentioned working here in the Keys, and after I gave it some thought, I decided it would be the perfect thing for me to do. Remember how I worked for Habitat that one summer during college? I called to see if they could use me for the next few weeks here. They said they'd love to have me, but didn't have the space. I told them I could share a room with my wife."

"You told them I was your wife?"

"They wouldn't let me stay in your room otherwise. I told them we had some issues, but we were both determined to work them out." He told himself to look at it not as a lie, but as a stretched truth.

"We've already worked it out," Lillian said. "It's called a divorce." She put her carry-on down, closed her eyes, and took a deep breath. "I'm going to go get Tom."

"Don't do that, Lillian." He stood up, but hesitated to take a step toward her when she put her hand on the doorknob. She looked haggard and wary. "Come inside, take a shower, and rest for a bit. Then we'll talk. You look exhausted."

For a second, he thought she would ignore him. She had a defiant gleam in her eyes. But fatigue seemed to have caught with her, she dropped in a chair by the door.

"My flight from New York was delayed," she said. "And because of that, I ended up missing my connection in Miami. My options were to wait for a standby seat I probably wouldn't get or rent a car and drive."

"You drove from Miami?"

"In a car the size of a turnip."

"You don't drive."

"I don't drive often. There's a difference."

Not enough of one, in his opinion. "You should have called someone or taken a car service."

"Do you know what car service costs to get here from Miami?"

"No," he admitted. "But I know you can afford to call one." Hell, he'd given her a ten figure settlement in the divorce. She hadn't gone through it in less than three years, had she?

"You know nothing about my finances."

He stopped himself before asking what she meant by that. Obviously, she was trying to bait him into an argument and he wouldn't succumb. "Of course," he said instead. "You're right and it's not my business. The bottom line is, it scares me you had to drive."

She said nothing further nor did she try to continue their argument. Maybe he should agree and tell her she was right more often.

"But," he said, hoping he wasn't tempting fate. "You have to agree that you're running on fumes, and that you'll feel better after a nice long shower. So before you decide what you want to do or where you want to go from here, why don't you take a minute or two to yourself?"

She stood and unzipped her bag, taking from it a toiletry bag he recognized and a handful of clothing. "I'm locking the bathroom door."

"I'd never think about invading your privacy like that."

She raised an eyebrow. "That might be the stupidest thing I've ever heard you say. Especially considering the current situation. It didn't escape my attention there's only one bed in here."

He almost told her he was aware of that fact there was only one bed. After all, it wasn't anything he could either deny or pretend he didn't see. He wisely stayed silent. She shot him a nasty glare as she walked past him and into the bathroom. The door clicked, locked.

Fuck, he had a feeling he'd screwed this up.

LILLIAN LOOKED about a million times more relaxed when she stepped out of the bathroom forty-five minutes later. He was glad one of them was more relaxed. After listening to the shower run for who-knows-how-long and imaging Lillian in there, naked, all wet and surrounded by steam, he was hard as a damn rock.

"You look as if you feel better," he said, trying not to grit his teeth as he talked. A hard task, watching as she walked into the main part of the cabin. Her hair was still wet, dripping at the ends. His mind flashed back to an image, years prior, of her hair dripping on his chest as she rode him in bed after a shower. The feel of those cool droplets of water splashing on his hot skin...

Fuck.

"Ty?" She raised an eyebrow while towel drying her hair.

"Hmm?"

"Are you okay?" She asked. "You look like you're in pain."

He shifted in his seat at the small desk he where he sat. "It's nothing."

But they'd known each other far too long and far too well for her to believe him. She glanced down at his groin.

"Doesn't look like nothing to me," she said with an evil grin.

"Let me rephrase," he said. "It's nothing you need to concern yourself with."

"Trust me," she quipped. "Your dick doesn't concern me in the least."

"I didn't expect it would. That's why I didn't say anything."

She sighed and sat down on the side of the bed, close to the desk he was at. If he wanted, he could reach his hand out and touch her knee. But he knew she wouldn't welcome his touch, and he vowed to himself not to touch her again until she begged.

He cleared his throat, wanting to get out the rest of what he had to tell her. "There's another reason I'm here."

"You mean other than to annoy the shit out of me?"

He gave her a small grin at the I'm completely serious joke, but he knew it didn't reach his eyes, and that more than likely, she'd realize something else was going on.

"Is something wrong?" She stopped drying her hair and placed the towel in her lap. "Why the somber look all of a sudden?"

Of course something was wrong, they weren't together. It was the biggest wrong there was. But that wasn't what she meant. And it wasn't what he wanted to talk about at the moment.

"I had an appointment this morning," he said. "That's why I came in yesterday, and why I'm not part of the volunteer group today." She hadn't asked about his presence here at the campground, while everyone else was working.

"What kind of appointment?"

He wasn't sure how she'd respond to his answer. If she'd be glad or thought he was wasting his time. Either way, she should know his intentions. "I still have no memory of....that night. But there's a specialist in Key West who was highly recommended. I had a consultation with her earlier today. She thinks she can help me get parts of it back."

"Hypnosis?" Lillian asked.

"Something like that."

"Why would you do that?"

Lilian had never been a believer in hypnosis, claiming it was nothing but smoke and mirrors.

"Because I need to know what happened," he said.

"I've always thought what happened was obvious."

"Yes, but — "

"Ty, stop. We've been through this. There were no traces of drugs found anywhere. Not in any of the barware, the drinks, nothing. You were tested, too, and everything came back clean."

He couldn't argue with anything she said. Yes, they had tested everything, including him, and found nothing to explain his lapse in memory. But that didn't change the fact he still had a hole in his head where the memory of that night should be.

"I can't stop," he told her. "I have to know what happened. Can't you see? I lost everything over a night I can't remember."

She sucked in a breath at his words.

Why, he wondered? Because he only referred to himself and didn't say they had lost everything? He'd thought about it, but didn't want to assume she felt the same.

"I get it," she said. "I do."

"Do you?" He arched an eyebrow at her.

"I've decided not to rat you out to Tom," she said. "Though I'll have you know my plan was to have a torrid affair this week and having you here will put a damper on things."

It took him a second or two to realize she was joking. "Yeah," he said. "I can see how difficult it could be to bring a man into the cabin you're sharing with your ex-husband."

"You aren't even going to be known as my ex-husband for the next two weeks. You told them we were married."

He kept to himself that if he had it to do over, he'd do the same thing again. "Give me these two weeks, Lillian. Give us these two weeks. Not for me to win you over or to try to make you change your mind, but to be us. Let's put the past aside and work together to help those in need."

CHAPTER 7
LILLIAN

As Lillian walked with Ty to the main building for dinner a few hours later, she couldn't stop thinking about him undergoing hypnosis in order to recall the events of that night. She had to admit, when he first told her he had no memories about anything that had happened, she didn't believe him. Sure, he couldn't remember. Right. She wasn't born yesterday.

But he never waved, and when he called his doctor and ask for him to run a toxicity screen, she started thinking maybe someone had slipped a little something in his drink.

Then the results came back and showed nothing. They had found no trace of anything on the items submitted. Though Ty continued in his insistence something had to have been done, Lillian found it harder and harder to believe. She couldn't understand how it was possible for both him and his assistant to get naked in front of each other, then do God knows what in her bed, and him not remember a bit.

Torn between whether or not to believe Ty, Lillian reached out to the other guests who had been at the party that night. Isaac had been out of town on business, but Lance had attended, and he brought with him the woman he'd been seeing at the time, Sabrina. Sabrina was also a senior at Juilliard, and the recipient of the annual scholarship given by Lance's family.

Franky, Lillian had thought it a bit questionable for the two of them to be dating, but it wasn't her place to judge. Besides, if Barbra Murphy, Lance's grandmother, founder and head of the scholarship foundation, didn't seem to have a problem with it, Lillian shouldn't either. Not that it mattered to a hill of beans anymore, since Lance was now dating a woman who'd also won the scholarship. Although to be fair, she had declined it eventually.

Regardless, while at the party that fateful night, Lance received a call from his attorney about several copyright issues concerning a gala Barbara had in the works. He ended up leaving early, but Sabrina wasn't ready to go when he was, so they agreed for her to stay. Ty ensured Lance that he'd see to it personally that Sabrina made it home safely.

No two partygoers had the same story about what happened next. A few weren't observant enough to have noticed anything beyond themselves and their own little world. Among those who claimed to know what happened, relatively little was consistent between them.

. . .

Lillian heard the sound of voices as they approached the main building, pulling her back to the present. Her heart pounded. Could she pull off two weeks of pretending to be married to Ty? Forget pulling it off, more importantly, could she mentally handle two weeks of pretending to be married to him?

She suspected that in leaving New York and coming to Florida, she'd jumped from the frying pan headfirst into the fire. She'd left to get away from him and to do something atypical in order to keep her mind off of him, and now she faced two weeks of sharing the same room with him. The irony would have made her laugh if she wasn't the one actually living it.

She couldn't decide if the current situation made her stupid, naïve, or just sad.

"Why so serious?" Ty asked.

"I don't know if I can do this."

"Dinner?"

"No." She punched his arm. "You and me and this whole two week thing."

He nodded. "For now, let's just do dinner."

She didn't like doing that, pretending like there wasn't a problem when clearly there was one, and everyone saw it. But right this very second, steps away from the door of a building that held the people they'd be working with over the next two weeks, was not the time to get into a deep discussion with her ex.

No doubt they'd have plenty of time to hash out anything they wanted to over the coming days.

She sighed. "Okay."

Ty pushed open the door to the main building, and they stepped inside. Off to one side, a half wall separated the small dining area from the rest of the cabin. At the moment its tables and chairs were filled with diners, eleven she estimated. Though they all seemed to be talking and not eating.

"Are we late?" she asked out of the corner of her mouth.

"I don't think so," Ty replied. "By my watch we left our cabin early."

That's what she'd thought, too, but that didn't explain all the people sitting at the tables.

"There you two are."

Lillian and Ty both turned to find Tom standing off to the side.

"Are we late?" Lillian asked.

Tom shook his head. "No, I forgot to tell you two that everyone congregates in this building before dinner."

That explained why no one was eating. There were noticeably more men than women, seven and three, but that made sense.

"Is this everyone?" she asked. She thought it probably was. According to the website, the total number of people working in any group would be limited. She preferred small groups. They were more personal, allowing you to get to know each other better. Or that had always been her thought, anyway.

Smaller groups were also more intimate, but that wasn't a word she thought wise to use around Ty. Though she'd wished she'd thought about a brief fling before she allowed him to stay in her room. It would be nice to have sex again.

Another thing she would not be telling Ty. Besides, the one and done lifestyle had never been her thing. If other people wanted to sleep around, okay for them. Assuming, she felt the need to add, that no one was married to someone else.

"Almost, everyone," Tom said in reply to her question. "I don't see EJ yet. He's the site manager. He should be here soon. We really lucked up. He's only able to get away from his office and help in person once a year or so. Most of the time, he works with us remotely."

"What does he do?" Ty asked.

"What doesn't he do?" Tom replied and then chuckled. "He says he's an architect, but I think he has as few other degrees he's hiding."

"Sounds like he's a handy guy to have around," Ty said.

"He is. I'll introduce you later. " Tom nodded toward the dining room. "Looks like it's time to eat."

They soon found themselves sitting and eating with the other volunteers. Everyone was warm and inviting. There was one other couple, a group of three recent college grads, and the remaining five were from the same small business.

"Team building on crack," A woman with the business group, said with a snort. Lillian soon learned that she was the owner of the business.

The three college graduates reminded her so much of Lance, Isaac, and Ty at their age. She could imagine the three of them doing something similar if the opportunity would have provided itself.

The man and woman who made up the other couple were friendly, but didn't join in the conversation much. All Lillian learned about them was that they had retired recently.

After dinner, they were all to meet in the main room to discuss the new project they were starting the next day. Lillian and Ty cleared their places and were getting ready to find a seat, when Tom called out to them.

"Mr. and Mrs. Bancroft," the older man said. "Come over here. I want you to meet EJ."

Lillian turned back around with a big smile, excited to meet the man who impressed Tom so much. Her face froze at the sight of him.

"Fucking hell," Ty said.

EJ was Eric the Dom.

CHAPTER 8
TY

If there had been any doubt in Ty's mind that the universe hated him, seeing the Dom Lillian made a connection with days earlier, standing in front of him in Florida would have crushed it like a bug.

"Lillian," Eric said, his mouth open in shock, but obviously thrilled to see her again. "I didn't expect to see you here."

"Ditto," Lillian replied in a stunned voice.

Eric looked at Ty and narrowed his eyes. "Mr. and Mrs. Bancroft?"

Ty shrugged. He wasn't going to tell the man anything.

"Lillian?" Eric asked.

She waved her hand, dismissing the unasked *I-thought-you-called-him-your ex-husband* question. "It's a long story."

"That appears to be a recurring theme for you," Eric replied with a half smile.

"It's a gift," Lillian replied.

Damn it all to hell and back. She was teasing him.

"I see you guys already know each other," Tom said, thankfully interrupting the happy reunion scene.

"I think saying we know each other is a stretch," Ty said. "It's more along the lines of we know of each other."

"Either way. I'm glad you're here," Eric said, but he only looked at Lillian when he spoke. "If you'll excuse me, I'll get everyone together and we'll go over our project for the next few days."

Lillian nodded, a serine smile on her face as Eric walked toward the front of the small gathering. Tom was at his side before Eric could address the small group, and they spoke in low voices no one could hear. Since everyone was still chatting, Ty leaned his head toward Lillian.

"Did you know he was going to be here?" he asked.

"Are you really asking me that question?" She didn't turn her head to look at him.

"I think I just did. Don't you think it's questionable the two of you happened to meet in Manhattan days before you arrive in the Florida Keys for a project he's the site manager on?" He spoke to the side of her head, because she still refused to look at him. "I think it sounds like stalking if you ask me."

"Well, I didn't ask you." She said without moving her head. "And no, it doesn't sound like stalking. It sounds like destiny."

Destiny, his ass.

Eric asked for everyone's attention, and as the group grew silent, Ty couldn't help but look at and assess Eric.

This was the man Tom thought was so wonderful? Eric, the talented. Eric, the architect. Eric, the Dom. To Ty he looked like Eric, the ordinary. Ty didn't think Eric was a stalker, but you could never know with any certainty what people might be capable of doing. Appearance could fool anyone. Maybe he'd give Eric's name to Isaac and have his business partner look into him. If the architect Dom was going to be spending time with Lillian, someone had to ensure it was safe for her to be around him.

He needed Eric's last name. Surely, he could get it from Tom.

"Anyone have questions?" Eric asked from the front of room.

Ty realized he'd tuned the man out and had no idea what they were doing or where they were going tomorrow. Maybe someone would ask a question.

But the seconds ticked by and no one raised their hand or spoke. Ty couldn't believe it, there was always a person in every group with a plethora of dumb ass questions to ask. That guy. The one that made everyone roll their eyes whenever he opened his mouth.

"In that case," Eric said. "Sleep well, and I'll catch you guys bright and early in the morning. If you're riding the van, be sure to eat breakfast first. Wheels on the road at seven-thirty."

Everyone headed to their cabins. Ty noticed Lillian yawning as they walked back. Their cabin was on at the end of the row. It wasn't much of a walk, but the heat and mosquitos made it feel one hundred times longer.

He slapped at one of the blood suckers snacking on his neck. "I forgot to bring bug spray."

"I brought some." Lillian stifled another yawn. "You can use mine."

"If I know you," he said. "It's some all natural, organic, doesn't-work-like-crap spray you paid out the nose for."

"Fine. Let the bugs eat you alive. It's that or nothing."

"Using that is the same as using nothing." Ty opened the cabin door for Lillian to enter. She tried to talk but yawned instead, and he couldn't make out a word she said. He chuckled and nudged her toward the bed. "Go to sleep. You're exhausted. I promise I'll let you insult me in the morning."

She gave a sleepy nod. "Okay. Where are you going to sleep?"

"I'll be fine on the floor." She would have to ask him back into her bed. He wasn't bringing it up, and he wasn't asking.

He let her into the bathroom first, and by the time he finished she was already sleeping.

TY GROANED as he got to his feet the next morning. He was getting too old to sleep on the floor, was his first thought. His second was, when had he turned into such a damn wuss? It was still early, just after five, but he knew he'd never be able to go back to sleep. If he was in London, he'd go for a jog, and if he was in New York, he'd visit the gym Lance and Isaac had added to the office.

But he wasn't in London or New York. He was in Florida, and already it was much too hot to jog, and he doubted the old resort had a gym.

Lillian was still sleeping after he made a quick trip to the bathroom and changed. Being as quiet as he could, he crept out of the cabin, making sure the door closed softly behind him.

As soon as he stepped outside, the humidity descended on him. Even so, he needed coffee. He wasn't sure if anyone else would be up yet, but surely he could find a coffee marker in the area where they had dinner the night before.

The smell greeting him when he opened the door to the main cabin told him someone else was up and had the same idea as he'd had. Good. That meant he wouldn't have to wait for it to make.

He stepped inside, prepared to give whoever it was a big thank you. Surprisingly, only one person was visible. And of fucking course it was Eric the Great.

He didn't let the man's presence deter him from his coffee goal. Last night, while Lillian was in the bathroom before going to bed, Ty had sent all the information he had on Eric to Isaac. Isaac told him he'd lost it, but didn't push his point when Ty replied that yes, he had lost it, but he was doing everything in his power to get it back.

With the confidence that he'd soon know all of Eric's secrets, he put on a big smile, and when the other guy looked his way, Ty nodded.

"Good morning," Ty said. Coffee smells good."

"I made plenty. Go grab a cup."

Minutes later, coffee in hand, Ty went over his options. Go back to the cabin and risk waking Lillian. Sit outside in the heat and drink hot coffee. Or suck it up and make small talk.

He and Eric the Great were going to be spending a lot of time together in the next few weeks. It'd be in everyone's best interest for that time to go by as smoothly as possible.

Ty walked over to the table where Eric was. "Mind if I sit here?"

Eric looked up from his phone. "Not at all."

"Are you always an early riser?" Ty asked. Not because he cared or wanted to know, but because someone had to say something, and it was only five-thirty.

"I suppose I am," Eric said. "I've never had to set an alarm, which is good in some ways, but it also means I rarely sleep past six. Are you usually up this early?"

"I have been since my move back to the States a few weeks ago." He smiled. "I can't decide if it's the world's worst case of jet lag or if I'm just getting old."

"We'll go with jet lag. You and I can't be that far apart in age, and I'm not ready for my body to start falling apart yet."

"Agreed."

They both sipped their coffee. Only a moment had passed before Eric asked, "You said you've only been back in the States for a few weeks. Where were you living before?"

"I was in London for nearly three years."

"Doesn't sound like you picked up an accent," Eric said with a grin.

Ty chuckled. "No, I didn't get that ingrained into the culture. My sister moved with me, so that might have also helped."

"Your sister?" Eric asked. "Lillian didn't go with you?"

Fucking hell, how had they found their way to this topic? "No, Lillian and I were divorced when I moved."

"Ah," Eric said, as if solving a great mystery. "So you actually are her ex-husband."

"Yes," was the only reply he gave.

"I wasn't sure if I should believe what Lillian told me at the club or if I should go with what Tom said."

"Lillian doesn't lie. Ever," Ty said, making sure Eric understood. "Anything she tells you, you can take to the bank."

Eric said nothing for several long seconds.

"I'm the one who told Tom we were married," Ty added. No reason not tell him, it was the truth. One Eric could have discovered with a single question to Tom. "I guess I still see her as mine."

But she's not.

Eric didn't say it. He didn't have to. The three words were clear in his expression when he took a sip of coffee.

CHAPTER 9
LILLIAN

It didn't surprise her when Ty asked if they could take her rental to the site rather than riding the bus. He'd told her earlier a hired car service brought him in from the airport.

"Have you seen my rental?" she asked. "I'm not sure it can accommodate you, much less both of us."

He rolled his eyes, suggesting she assumed, he thought she was exaggerating about the car's size. Instead of arguing, she decided to let him find out for himself. They ate a quick breakfast and headed to where she'd parked the day before. The other couple in the group also had a rental. The recent college grads and the small business group rode the van Eric drove.

"I ran into Eric when I went out looking for coffee earlier, while you were still sleeping," Ty said. "I asked him for directions."

"So you know how to get to where we're going, but do you know what we're going to do once we arrive there?" She couldn't help but ask.

Ty hesitated just a second too long, and she knew her thoughts concerning the night before were correct.

She came to a stop we they reached the car. "You don't have a clue what we're doing today, do you?"

But his attention wasn't on their conversation. He stared in horror at the vehicle before him. "Please, God, tell me this is not your rental."

She couldn't fault him for changing the subject since the car was so shockingly small, but she made a note to return to the previous topic later.

"The guy at the rental counter said it'd get good gas mileage," she said.

"Only because you have to pedal it with your feet." He walked to the passenger side and opened the door for her to get in. "We'll have to make it work. The van's already left, and it looks like the empty nesters are pulling out now."

Ty managed to get himself seated. "I just sent you a text with the directions. Can you navigate?"

It was so similar to what they used to do when they were younger. Going off for the weekend with only a change of clothes and a map. Lillian would always be the navigator because even though he was brilliant, Ty couldn't read a map to save his life.

One summer, while still in college, they attended a wedding in Florence, South Carolina. Neither of them had been there before, and even though Florence was in the northern part of the state, they decided to rent a car after the festivities were over and drive south to spend a few days in Charleston.

The weekend of the wedding came, and Ty had a few drinks at the reception. Though he appeared fine, they both agreed it would be best for Lillian to drive. She turned the navigation over to Ty. Everything was fine until they hit a major back up on the interstate. Ty grabbed the map the rental agency gave them and, after several minutes of studying it, announced he'd found a shortcut.

Something didn't seem right about Ty's shortcut. They drove through several small towns where the speed limit dropped so low, Lillian couldn't help but think the interstate would have been faster. Traffic back up and all.

Of course, Ty disagreed and told her to trust him because he knew what he was doing. She hadn't replied, but he told her he could see the doubt in her eyes. At that point she told him to shut up and focus on the map.

It wasn't until they saw the Welcome to North Carolina signs that Lillian told Ty he was never to touch a map again. They'd ended up in a crap hotel on the border. Lillian swore she'd never forgive him if she didn't end up getting to eat some of Charleston's famous she-crab soup.

Her heart ached to remember that carefree couple, laughing at life and arguing over radio stations. Content with the world and each other. How had that couple turned into who they were today?

"Lillian?" Ty asked, and she realized she hadn't answered. "Can you navigate?"

"Yes," she replied, reaching for her phone and scrolling through her texts. "Got it."

But they'd been together for far more years than they'd been apart, and he knew her too well.

He placed his hand on the top of her knee. "Are you okay?"

His touch wasn't sexual at all. Instead, it felt comforting. She'd forgotten that part of him. Either that or she'd purposely set it aside any time it came to mind in order to force herself to forget. She closed her eyes against the onslaught of memories flooding her mind. How safe she'd been in his arms. How strong they'd felt around her, and how being surrounded by that strength always made her feel strong.

"I was just thinking about the time you navigated us to Charleston from Florence via North Carolina," she told him. Between the story of their past and how his touch made her feel, the story was the safest confession.

"God, you were so mad," he said with a laugh. "I felt like the world's biggest idiot, and you didn't talk to me until we finally made it to Charleston the next day."

He didn't have to remind her what happened next. She'd taken a long shower once they were in their hotel room. When she stepped out of the bathroom, she discovered he'd had the room's private deck transformed into a romantic table for two, complete with twinkling lights and crisp linens. He then served her the best she-crab soup she'd ever had.

Lillian tried to keep her mind from thinking about what happened after dinner, but the traitorous organ remembered all to well how lovingly and passionately he'd made love to her that night.

"Why did we never go back to Charleston?" she asked him. It seemed odd now that she thought about it. There had been so many things they'd wanted to do and see, but weren't able to fit into that one weekend. While exploring the area, they'd often talked about adding something to the list for when they returned, but they'd never made it back.

"Maybe because subconsciously we knew it'd never be the same," he said. "Or wouldn't measure up to what we remembered, and we didn't want to tarnish what we had or to replace those memories with something inferior."

"I suppose so," she said. On some level it made sense, but not on others. You didn't refuse a second experience because the first one was so fantastic. She didn't stop going to her favorite restaurant because she feared the chef was having an off day.

"Okay, you were right," Ty said, dragging her away from her thoughts.

"Trying to sweet talk me?" She lowered her head and peered at him over the top of her sunglasses. "Are you after something?"

"Me?" he asked as if it was the most ridiculous thing he'd ever heard. "Trust me, if I was after something from you, one, there would be no doubt what I was after, and two, you'd be willing to give it to me." Before she could take a breath to tell him to get over himself, he continued, "All I'm doing is admitting you were correct with your assumption earlier that I have no idea what we're doing today."

His admission shocked her so much, she couldn't come back a sassy reply. "Oh?"

"Yeah," he said. "I was too caught up how much of a stalker I thought Eric was to listen to what he was talking about."

She bit back her remark that between the two men, Ty was the one who acted more like a stalker. They'd had that argument the night before and she didn't want to relive it. "We're going to repair a home the last hurricane damaged. It's not enough to condemn the house, but enough to make it inhabitable. It's owned by a widow with three young kids."

"Insurance isn't covering it?"

"Her late husband had let the policy lapse, and she didn't know. The home was previously owned by his parents and was paid off." Lillian shook her head. "From what I heard, it's only been seven months or so since the husband passed away. Hard to imagine going from the relief of not having a mortgage to the horror at realizing it didn't matter because you didn't have insurance and now you can't live in your home. They're basically homeless."

"How old are the kids?"

"One, three, and five if CEO is right," she said.

"CEO?"

She nodded. "That's what I'm calling the lady who owns the small business. We chatted this morning on the way to breakfast."

He nodded, and she knew him well enough to guess he was probably thinking of the now single mother of three. Her and her children and making their home into something habitable. Lillian hoped his relationship with her and all the burdens of their shared history could be put aside for now. Maybe he was a big enough person to be around Eric and not act petty and jealous. Or maybe he'd be so busy with the work he was doing, Lillian wouldn't even cross his mind.

She swallowed her snort, because she knew he was telling herself a lie.

CHAPTER 10
LILLIAN

Lillian couldn't help but notice how quiet Ty became after she gave him the details of their project. It didn't surprise her, he'd always been quick to step in when someone needed help.

Ty pulled up to the project site where the other volunteers were spilling out of the van. More likely than not, based on what Eric had said the night before, this would be the only location the group worked at for most, if not all, of her stay. Eric looked up and waved the two of them over, along with the retired couple who arrived moments after they did.

"How'd we beat them?" Ty asked Lillian in a whisper. "They left before we did."

"He must have known a shortcut," was her reply. "I would say at least they didn't wind up in another state, but I don't think it'd be possible for anyone to navigate so poorly they'd be able to leave Florida and not know. Even you."

He shot her a smile. "Don't give me too much credit. I might surprise you with just how poor my navigational skills are."

They had reached the rest of their group by then and everyone circled around Eric. They weren't in a neighborhood. In fact, there weren't any other houses nearby. Based on the way the ground sank and made squishing sounds wherever she stepped, it wasn't hard to see why no one else had built in this area.

Eric began by going through the many things that need to be done and the order in which they should do them. Initially, he was sending half the group to work on the home's foundation, while the other half started inside on the carpeting and flooring.

Ty went with the foundation group and Lillian joined those working inside. It would be hotter than hell no matter which group she went with, but at least inside she wouldn't have the sun beating down on her or have to worry about getting sunburn. She stopped herself from asking Ty if he put any sunscreen on and if so, what SPF he had used. He was a grown ass man. He had known there was a good chance of having to work outside and should have prepared accordingly. It wasn't her concern or worry.

Eric spoke to the lady she'd dubbed CEO and then headed over to the other group. Lillian supposed it'd be a good idea to call CEO by her actual name, Liza, in her head. If not, there was the potential of her calling her CEO out loud.

Liza pulled them over to the side of the house.

"As you can see," she said, waving her hand toward the house behind her. "This is a one-story ranch. The floors have substantial water damage and most of what's in there is carpet. First thing we have to do is to rip it all out to see what exactly we're dealing with. The hope is we'll be able to put in hardwood flooring throughout most of the house."

She spoke briefly about safety. "It's the mom in me. Sorry," she said with a grin. "I know we're all adults here. Grab a pair of gloves and let's get busy."

WHEN TOM PULLED up to the worksite four and a half hours later with boxed lunches donated by a local deli, Lillian had never been more ready for a break. She hadn't expected the work to be easy, but from the way her back and muscles already ached, she'd vastly overestimated her body's ability.

She took her lunch and walked to an empty makeshift table someone created from plywood and sawhorses. The table looked sturdy enough, but the chair? Not so much. She looked around to see what Ty was up to and was pleasantly surprised to find him eating and chatting with one of the recent college grads. Grant, she thought his name was.

Apparently, Ty wouldn't insist on sticking to her like glue. She should be happy he didn't want to be her shadow. Why wasn't she?

"If you're worried over the stability of the chairs," a deep voice said from beside her. "Tom brought them from his place and I can vouch for them."

She turned to find Eric standing and holding one of the lunches. "Hi Eric and thanks. I was a little leery about sitting down."

"Mind if I join you?"

She really didn't want company for lunch, she'd much rather have enjoyed a few quiet moments with her own thoughts. Though many viewed her as a people person, mostly it was all an act. And an exhausting act at that. But her earlier glance had shown her that this was the only table with empty chairs. It wouldn't be right to send him off to sit on a dead tree stump to balance his lunch on his knees while attempting to eat.

"Not at all," she said with what she hoped was a convincing smile. "Have a seat."

"Thanks." He sat down and unpacked the sandwich, chips, and apple from the box. "How's your first day going?"

"Very humbling." She picked up her sandwich and took the tomato out. "I learned I'm nowhere near as fit as I thought I was."

He chuckled. "Typical for the first day. It's not that you aren't in shape, it's that you're using muscles you typically don't. Take it easy this afternoon and make sure you take something if you need to when we get back. Did you bring anything?"

"Yes, I'm good." She always traveled with a small bottle of over-the-counter pain relief, and she'd double checked her bag before leaving New York to make sure they were there. "How long did it take for your muscles to stop hurting?"

"Who said they have?" His eyes danced with mischief.

They both laughed, and he told her about his first time as a volunteer and all the things he did wrong. He was naturally funny, and she hadn't realized how much time had passed until he checked his watch and indicated it was time to get back to work.

"Lillian," he said, as she gathered her trash to throw away. "I'd really like to get to know you better, and I know it's a bit awkward with you sharing a cabin with your ex-husband and everything , but will you go out to dinner with me? No pressure, it's just we have many of the same interests, and I'll admit it, you intrigue me."

By many of the same interests, she assumed he meant since she was a sub and he was a Dom. She probably should turn him down.

But she hesitated.

You intrigue me.

In that moment, the truth hit her. He intrigued her as well.

And, she told herself, that didn't have to mean anything. It could be exactly what it was without pretense or explanation.

This wasn't forever. Not even close. It was just dinner with a man she'd admitted to herself on several occasions that she was attracted to. A man who admitted that he was attracted to her. Simple attraction. That their sexual needs were similar was secondary.

She ripped up the train tracks on that thought process very quickly. Sex wasn't on the menu here. It wasn't even served in the restaurant. She hadn't had sex since the divorce, and she didn't envision Eric being the one to end her dry spell.

But he could, her body whined. If she let him. If she gave the slightest hint of interest, there was no doubt he'd jump at the chance to reintroduce and reeducate her on carnal pleasure. Her belly tightened at the thought. Of having sex again or having sex with Eric? She didn't take the time to determine the answer.

Ty would no doubt hate the idea of her going to dinner with Eric, and would pitch high holy hell when she told him, but that wasn't her fault. His reactions weren't her problem or concern.

"Looks like a lot of thought going into the answer for a simple question," Eric said, but Lillian didn't answer. "Lillian, listen, if you're not attracted to me or if you don't want to go out and spend time with me, just say so, and I'll never bother you again. And I promise, I can take it, and not be a jerk about it. But I want to know more about you, and maybe I'm being prideful, but I think you want to spend time and perhaps get to know me as well."

ALL OR NONE

She could take his word to the bank. She knew that much about him. If she told him she wasn't interested in him at all, he'd nod, tell her goodbye and that would be the end of it.

It would be so easy to tell him no. One breath and it'd be done. One breath.

But she didn't want to tell him no. She wanted to get to know him better, and God help her, she might even be willing to go as far as exploring their similar interests together.

"Dinner would be lovely," she said. "When were you thinking?"

Erics's face lit up in excitement. "I was thinking tomorrow night, if that would work for you?"

"Tomorrow night would be perfect."

CHAPTER 11
LILLIAN

At the job site the next day, everything on the surface appeared to be the same. But one didn't have to look hard to see the undercurrent churning and its ability to change everything. Lillian didn't have to look for it, she was living it.

Ty had still been in a pissy mood that morning, and she'd done her best to ignore him. She'd given serious thought to riding the van, but decided that would be childish. He was a grown man, and he'd just have to find a way to deal with the fact that she wasn't his anymore. He'd had plenty of time in London, she couldn't figure out why it seemed like such an issue now. She didn't think for a minute he'd been celibate the entire time he was overseas.

So it was a tension filled day. At least to her, anyway. It wasn't as bad when they were working. That was enough to keep her mind occupied and off of the two men. But whenever there was a break and during lunch, she felt both sets of eyes on her. She was thankful Eric ate with some of the other guys and didn't ask to sit with her again.

Part of the reason he did so might have been because Lillian started up a conversation with Penny, one half of the retired couple, as soon as lunch was announced and ended up sitting next to her and her husband.

Ty was quiet on the way back to the resort after they called it a day, which wasn't like him at all. Lillian breathed a sigh of relief when, after parking the car, he said he'd planned to talk with one of the college grads about employment opportunities overseas. She'd hadn't been looking forward to getting ready for a date with him in the cabin, scowling the entire time.

Shake it off, she told herself. It was his choice to follow her here; she hadn't forced him to come. It wasn't her responsibility to keep him entertained, and for damn sure she would not change the way she lived her own life for fear of upsetting him.

AT SIX-THIRTY ON THE DOT, Eric knocked on the cabin's door. Lillian took one last look at her reflection in the bathroom mirror. She'd have to do. In a moment of ridiculousness while packing, she'd thrown a casual sundress - from the back of her closet, aka a brightly colored one - in her bag. She didn't think she'd have the opportunity to wear it, but you never knew, and it was always a good idea to be prepared. Of course, her preparations hadn't extended far enough to makeup, which meant all she had with her was loose powder and a few tubes of lipstick.

Eric's gaze took her in when she opened the door. "You look incredible," he said.

She felt her cheeks heat. How long had it been since a man complimented her on the way she looked? So long she couldn't remember. "You don't look half bad yourself."

And he didn't. His hair was still a little damp from his recent shower, and he'd changed from the blue jeans and SPF shirt he wore at the job site into a crisp pair of tan shorts and a blue collared shirt matching the color of his eyes.

"How does seafood sound?" he asked once he'd helped her into the truck he'd rented, and they were on the main road.

"Sounds divine," she replied, and her stomach growled in response. "I haven't had any seafood since I got here."

"We can't have that. There's this little out of the way place I know of, and you'll love it."

"I know nothing about the area. I'm in your hands." As soon as the phrase was out of her mouth, she realized how it sounded. "I mean...." Damn her stupid mouth.

Eric didn't turn to look at her, but she saw his smile. "Not totally," he said. "Not yet anyway."

She waited for a twinge of arousal to warm her body, but nothing of the sort happened. Instead of dwelling on why, she chalked it up to the after effects of two days spent laboring in the sun. Surely, she'd react differently when she was more rested. Though that didn't explain why she didn't feel tired at the moment.

If Ty had said something similar to her, would her body react differently? Would the same words spoken in his voice have the power to arouse her? She wanted the answer to be a resounding no, but in her mind, she heard Ty say, 'Not yet anyway,' in that seductive Dom voice of his. The resulting shiver down her back showed something different.

But, she tried to convince herself, it was only different in that she knew Ty better and had been intimate with him. It was the familiarity of Ty that made her body react. Nothing else. Even in her head it sounded like an illogical argument and made no sense at all, but that was what she was going with for now.

Not long after, Eric pulled up to a building that looked almost like the widow's house they were working on. Not quite as bad, but enough to make her question if it was open. And she would have asked Eric if there hadn't been so many cars parked outside. So many they suggested there was something of interest going on inside.

He didn't miss her raised eyebrow when he walked around to her side of the truck to help her down. "You're in my hands, remember?" he whispered. "Trust me."

The inside of the restaurant surprised her. Though crowded, it was clean and neat. The decadent aroma from the kitchen had her tastebuds doing cartwheels.

"It's a seat yourself kind of place," Eric said, leading her to a corner table a busboy just finished cleaning. "Is this okay?"

The food smelled so good, and she was so hungry, she'd eat standing up if she had to. But all she said in response was, "This is perfect."

"I try to eat here at least once whenever I'm down this way." Eric opened his menu. "You really can't go wrong with anything here. It's all good."

A memory popped into her head at his words. She was with Ty in Amsterdam, sometime shortly after college graduation. Ty searched the city looking for patatje oorlog, a popular food an international student had mentioned he should try. "He said all the food was good, but the patatje oorlog was the best."

As it turned out, the dish in question consisted of French fries covered in ketchup, mayo, chopped raw onions, and peanut sauce. She'd thought it might be edible up until she heard about the peanut sauce. At that point, she informed Ty that he could eat all he wanted, she was going to pass, and he would have to brush his teeth before kissing her.

She forced the memory out of her head. Ty wasn't here, and they weren't together. Across the table, Eric was still looking over his menu. Hopefully, her journey back in time had been unnoticed.

"What's your favorite here?" she asked.

Eric placed his menu down. When he looked at her the way he was now, it was as if there was nothing in the world more important than the discussion they were having. "Without question, the crab stuffed snapper. They don't use any breadcrumbs for the stuffing, it's mostly fresh crabmeat."

Lillian smiled and closed her menu. "You had me at crab stuffed."

"An excellent selection," he said, amusement clear in both his voice and eyes.

"Have you ever had she-crab soup from Charleston?"

"No," he said. "But I've always wondered why only the female crabs for soup? Do the males taste bad? And how can you be sure they didn't sneak a he crab in your soup?"

The question was both so unexpected and ridiculous, she sat stunned for the beat of a few seconds before giggling and saying, "I have no idea."

The server appeared to take their orders. Lillian went with the snapper and wasn't surprised when Eric did the same.

"Tom said you're an architect," Lillian said when they were alone again. "I don't think I've ever known an architect before."

"No matter how many times I tell him, he always leaves part of if off," Eric said with a grin. "It's not that he was totally wrong, but he wasn't totally right, either. I'm a remote solution architect. Not the type of architect most people have in mind. Basically, I work with code as opposed to blueprints."

"I see," she said. "You're one of those smart computer people. I'm always amazed at how much I don't know about information technology." It was the only thing she could think of to say other than never in one trillion years would she have pegged him as a computer guru.

"I don't know how smart I am, but I seem to do all right."

She had a feeling he was doing more than a little all right, but she didn't say it out loud. "Where do you live in real life?" she asked instead. "When you're not off repairing the homes of widows and fatherless children, that is."

It was a reasonable question. After all, she had first met him at The Club, and, as far as she knew, they didn't offer membership to many people who lived out of state.

"I have an apartment in Tribeca," he said, and that confirmed her assumption he was doing better than all right.

He lifted an eyebrow. "I assume, based on our first meeting, you live around the same area?"

"Yes," she answered, right as they delivered the snapper to their table.

Whatever conversation they were having stopped while they took the first bite of their fish. Both the fish and crab were deliciously fresh, and while she couldn't place the spice used to season everything with, she knew she'd never forget its taste.

"Oh, my God," Lillian said, after her initial taste. "That might be one of the best dishes I've ever had."

Eric chuckled at her expression. "Right?"

She took another bite and closed her eyes in bliss. "I'll never doubt you again."

"Be careful," he said. "I might hold you to those words."

She needed to watch herself around Eric. Something told her if she opened the door for him just a smidgen, in less time than it took to snap her fingers, he'd have her convinced to throw it wide open. Having done that once with Ty, she wasn't in a hurry to repeat the experience.

And, she further lectured herself, never for one minute could she forget Eric was a Dom. Because when it came right down to it, it wouldn't be his intellect, his apartment, or that he was an undeniably attractive man who spent his vacation helping those less fortunate that would draw her to him. Oh no. It'd be the Dom part of him she'd find irresistible.

That deep secret need he held in check so well, no one would ever discover it unless he revealed it to them. She knew about it, but only by happenstance. If she hadn't gone to The Club that night, if she hadn't met Eric until her arrival in Florida, would they still be sitting here tonight? When would he choose to mention his need to dominate? He would, wouldn't he?

Having no experience in the BDSM dating scene, she wasn't sure how things typically went. Maybe Eric wouldn't have asked her to dinner if they hadn't met in a place that laid bare their mutual interest.

"Are you okay?" Eric asked.

She kicked herself for getting lost in her thoughts again. "Yes, of course."

"Sorry to imply you looked anything other than stunning, but you appeared a bit quizzical there for a second. Or your expression gave that impression."

"No, it's fine," she assured him, playing with the napkin in her lap. Might as well tell the truth from the beginning. For one, if she told the truth, she wouldn't have to remember any lies. Secondly, he was a Dom, and would find the truth out eventually, anyway. Best to start with it from the beginning. "I'm not offended. It's only this whole dating thing is new to me."

He looked surprised with her answer. "I thought your divorce was finalized some time ago?"

"It was," she confirmed. "I haven't been very active in the dating scene." She felt her cheeks heat. "Actually, it's more like I haven't been active at all."

His eyes grew so wide she feared they might pop out of his head. "You haven't dated since the divorce?"

Why did it sound so much worse when he said it as opposed to how it sounded in her head? "Until a few weeks ago," she said, hating she felt the need to justify her nonexistent dating record. "I worked as a personal assistant, and since my boss was a workaholic, I had little down time. When I had it, all I wanted to do was curl up with a book or sleep."

"Don't feel as if you need to explain anything." He reached across the table and brushed her hand with his fingertips. "But thank you for not turning me down."

His touch was soft and his words sincere. She found no fault in him, other than he wasn't who she wanted.

CHAPTER 12
TY

Ty paced to the front window of the cabin, peeked out, and paced back to the opposite wall. Lillian had left with Eric a little over an hour ago, and though it was too early for them to have returned, he couldn't stop himself from looking out to check every damn time he passed the window. He hadn't stepped a foot inside the cabin until he was certain the couple had left. Instead, he'd made himself busy, chatting with a few other of the volunteers and grabbing a leftover sandwich from lunch for his dinner.

The wrapped ham and cheese sat untouched on the small table in the cabin's living area. He couldn't bring himself to eat at the moment. Not while Lillian was out on a fucking date. With a Dom, no less. Ty took a deep breath, paced back to the widow, lifting the curtain again, just to be sure.

His phone vibrated in his pocket and he let the curtain fall back into place. He didn't want to talk with anyone, but on the off chance it was important, he pulled the phone out to check the display.

Isaac.

About damn time.

"Isaac," TY answered with. "What do you have for me?"

The guy he'd known for what felt like forever gave a half snort, half chuckle. "And a hello and good evening to you was well."

"Whatever." Ty was not in a mood to deal with Isaac being a smartass.

"I can tell you woke up on the wrong side of the bed this morning."

"Shows what you know," Ty said. "I didn't even sleep in a bed last night, and I don't think it's possible to wake up on the wrong side of the floor."

Isaac laughed on the other end of the line. "She put you on the floor? Classic Lillian."

Much as he liked Isaac, and as close as they were, Ty didn't want to discuss her with him. Partly because his friend knew more about the last few years of Lilian's life than Ty did. A fact that didn't sit too well with him at the moment.

"I couldn't blame her," Ty finally replied. "I'm thankful she's letting me sleep on her floor. She'd have been well within her rights to have kicked me out."

"True, but she'd never do that."

Which Ty also knew and had used that knowledge to his advantage. Not that it'd helped him at all so far, since Lillian was at that very moment out with another man. "No, she wouldn't," he agreed. "Now, tell me what you found out since I'm assuming you called me for that reason and not to be a pain in my ass."

"Correct," Isaac said. "Being a pain in your ass is just an added benefit."

Ty remained silent. Trying to get him to stop would have the opposite effect.

"Damn," Isaac said. "You used to be more fun."

Ty didn't tell him it was because Lillian made him fun, or that nothing had been fun since the divorce. "Get on with it," he said instead.

"Eric J. Barnes is completely clean," Isaac said. "No record of anything. Nothing criminal, no traffic violations, not even a parking ticket. He's about as clean as they come."

It was welcome news since Lillian was out with the guy at the moment, but damn, part of Ty wished Isaac had found something. An overdue library book. Something.

"And before you bug me," Isaac. said. "I asked around about him within the community."

Ty hadn't asked him to do so, but had expected he would. Just because someone had a clean public record didn't mean they were always a saint in private. "And?"

"He's been a member of the New York Club for two years. Before that, he was an active member at a sister club in

Chicago for five years. He's known as a sensual Dominant and again, no record of anything suspicious, no complaints from anyone he's ever played with. From what I found out, he's had one serious relationship, and it only ended because he got a promotion in Manhattan and the submissive he was with didn't want to move away from Chicago."

Fucking hell. Ty ran his free hand through his hair. "You've got to give me something. No one can be that perfect."

"Of course he's not perfect. He has flaws and shortcoming the same way we all do." Isaac hesitated for a second. "But I have to be honest when I say that if I had to pick out a guy for Lillian, Eric wouldn't be a terrible choice."

Isaac's words hit Ty square in the chest and for a second, he couldn't breathe. After a few seconds, he wheezed out, "What the fuck?"

"Lillian worked as my personal assistant the entire time you were in London, and she's like a sister to me. I want her to be happy, and if she can't find that with you, Eric doesn't look bad."

"She never gave us a chance," Ty said, finding it hard to believe Isaac could say such things. "She's the one who asked for a divorce."

"And you rolled over and played dead."

"What was I supposed to do? Force her to stay married?"

"No, but you could have at least fought for her. If you didn't sleep with that woman, you should have tried to make Lillian see the truth."

"What are you talking about?" Ty all but yelled. "I tried, damn it."

"Not the way I see it. From my perspective, you went off to London with your tail between your legs as fast as you could. I'm sorry, but sometimes the truth is hard to hear. Maybe a little tough love will do you some good. You gave up way too easily and way too quick."

"Fuck you, Isaac," Ty said before ending the call.

CHAPTER 13
LILLIAN

"Are you ready to head back, or would you like to go someplace else?" Eric asked after dinner and once they were back in his truck.

Dinner had been nice and Eric nothing but a gentleman, not that she had expected him to be anything else. But to be quite honest, she felt a bit torn. There was the side of her that knew Eric was a great guy, down to earth, and easy to talk with. Not to mention the volunteer work he did. That side of her whispered he was a catch and a half, and if she had a brain in her head, she would reel him in before someone else got their hooks in him.

"I'm not ready for the night to end yet," she said, which made the pro-Eric side of her happy. The other side, the more cynical and jaded side, whispered she only wanted to extend the date because she didn't want to return to the cabin where she'd have to face Ty. She told that side to sit the hell down and shut up.

"Me, either," Eric said with a smile, and Lord help her, he had a heart-stopping smile. "I know a place where can walk. It's not overrun with people, but it shouldn't be devoid of them, either. You'll be safe with me."

"A walk would be nice." It warmed her inside to watch how he looked at each situation from her perspective. How in this case he picked up on the fact she might feel uncomfortable walking in a private location with him. "How is it you're still single?" she could no longer stop herself from asking.

He laughed. "Well, if you ask my mom, it's because I turn down all the perfect online profiles of eligible women she sends me."

"Your mom sends you online profiles of single women?"

"Yes. But I think she only looks at their picture and nothing else. She's sent me a few real humdingers. And because she, obviously, doesn't know I'm a Dominant, I have a feeling most of them are vanilla."

Lillian wrinkled her brow. "I've been wondering how dating in the lifestyle worked."

"More often than not, I go out with women from The Club. That way I know they're in the lifestyle and won't dissolve into a fit of vapors when I mention kink."

"Has that happened before?"

"Only with women vetted by my mother," he said with a big grin. "She means well. She doesn't want me to be lonely, and I haven't been serious with anyone since moving from Chicago two years ago."

"Was there someone in Chicago?" Lillian asked.

"Yes, but she didn't want to move to New York, and I didn't want a long distance relationship, so we agreed to go our separate ways."

"That couldn't have been a simple decision for either of you to make."

"No, but not as hard as the one you made to leave Ty."

It had been a hard decision to make. "Few people understand that. I don't want to get into why we divorced, but I got the feeling everyone thought it should be easy to do."

"Of course it wasn't easy. You were married and expected to be married forever. There's nothing easy about deciding to end that."

His response was so similar to her own on the matter, she couldn't help but think she had been right the whole time.

He pulled into a public parking lot. There were two other cars parked, and when they made it down to the ocean, only a few people were visible off in the distance. They walked in silence for a bit.

Lillian couldn't help but think about that last statement Eric had made about expecting forever, and how correct he'd been. Maybe it was normal to need a lot of time to pass before heading back into the dating market following a divorce.

"Tell me how you got into kink," Eric said, no doubt thinking he was bringing up a lighter conversation than the one they'd just had.

Little did he know.

"Ty and I were invited to a party in college. I think our sophomore year. We had no idea anything like BDSM existed. We decided to try adding a little bit of kink at a time to our sex life. What can I say? We fell into the roles naturally, and we were hooked."

"I didn't know the two of you had been together that long," Eric said.

"We didn't get married until after we graduated, but yes, we were together for a long time."

Neither of them spoke for a few moments. Over the sound of the ocean, they weren't able to hear anyone else, even though there were a few people around.

"I assume then," Eric said, breaking the silence. "That Ty is the only man you've ever submitted to?"

She gave a weak laugh and tucked a wayward strand or hair behind her ear. "Is it that obvious?"

"Only because of the deer in the headlights look you gave me the night we met."

"Really?" she asked. Funny how she didn't remember feeling frightened or shocked that night.

"Yes," Eric said. "I would have thought you were a newbie if I hadn't been able to see the only thing you seemed to be in shock about was me approaching you. A newbie would have been watching everything other than me."

"It was my first time there as a single woman, or as in this case, a single submissive." She glanced up at him and saw he watched her intently. "You were also the only Dom who had ever approached me."

"I was probably the only one whoever interrupted Ty before."

"And," she added. "The only one whoever told him it appeared as if he was crossing the consent line."

"Ouch." Eric clutched his heart. "I bet that really shook him. But, I'd do it again the same way if I came across a similar scene."

"Of course, you would. That's why I like you."

He slowed his pace, and she did the same in order to keep up with him.

He stopped and turned to her. "I like you as well, Lillian."

CHAPTER 14
TY

As hour after hour passed and Lillian didn't return to the cabin, Ty grew more and more irritated. There was no way it took this long to eat dinner. He didn't care where they went. That being the case, the only thing Ty could assume was they'd went somewhere else when they finished eating, and since Eric was a Dom, Ty had a pretty good idea of what they were doing there.

Had Eric taken her back to his cabin? Ty hadn't thought of the possibility until that moment. Damn, he should have been watching Eric's cabin. Ty didn't know which cabin Eric stayed in, but there weren't that many. Surely it would be simple to figure out.

The thought of Eric touching Lillian made him want to vomit. Bad enough for it to be a vague thought when he was an ocean away and the man she was with nothing more than a hazy shadow, but it was exponentially worse when he'd seen what Eric looked like, knew what his voice sounded like. Both of those together and Ty's overactive imagination shot into overdrive.

The rattle of the cabin's doorknob forced him away from his thoughts and back to the situation at hand. It had to be Lillian. The only other person who had a key was Tom, and Ty assumed if a situation came up requiring the other man to use his key, he'd let whoever was inside know as opposed to barging in unexpectedly.

Lillian walked into the room. Her hair was in disarray and her cheeks were flushed a deep pink color. He couldn't pull his gaze from her. She looked glorious in an *I just got out of bed* way.

"Ty."

"That was a long dinner," he tried to keep his voice even, not wanting to come across as being accusatory.

"It was more than just dinner," she said matter-of-factly.

"Did you play with him?"

"I can't see how that's any of your business." She looked away and walked straight into the bathroom. He didn't hear the door lock, so he followed her.

She spun around, her gaze so fiery he swore he felt the flames. "What the hell are you doing in here?"

"I want to talk."

She put her hands on her hips. "So you followed me to the bathroom? Really?"

He opened his mouth to tell her she wasn't hiding anything he hadn't seen before, but in the second before he did, it hit him what she was wearing. A dress. A sundress.

Why would she have packed a sundress for two weeks of volunteer work?

"You're wearing a dress," he said, and she looked at him as if he'd lost his mind.

"Yes."

"Why did you pack a sundress?" It was a ridiculous question and one he had no business to ask. Lillian was an adult woman and had the right to pack anything she wanted. If she had a mind to pack an evening gown for her time in the Keys, she could do so without having to explain.

He fully expected her to tell him to go hang himself, but she took a step closer to him, looked him square in the face, and said, "Because I plan to fuck as many available men as possible for the next two weeks."

It took him a second to realize she was baiting him. She stood there with a smirk, knowing she'd got underneath his skin. He fisted his hands. "Trying to get a rise out of me?"

"There was no try involved."

"I should take you over my knee, flip up that skirt, and spank your ass for being such a brat." His words came out in a half hiss through clenched teeth.

"You wouldn't dare," she said, but he saw her eyes had grown dark and her breathing a bit choppy.

"Probably not," he said." But the idea I might turns you on."

She shook her head, and opened her mouth as though to argue, but before she got a word out, Ty placed a finger over her lips.

"Shh," he shushed her. "Don't make it worse by lying. I've known your body for too many years, and you can deny it or pretend it isn't so until you're blue in the face, but the one thing you can't do is lie to me."

In a move he hadn't expected, Lillian shifted her head slightly and sucked the tip of his finger into her mouth. Ty felt the pull all the way down to his dick. "Fuck, Lillian."

"Do it," she said in a coarse whisper. "Punish me. Punish me for thinking I could ever find anyone to replace you."

He pulled back. "Are you drunk?" She hadn't appeared to be when she walked into the room, but maybe she was hiding it somehow.

"No," she said, and he couldn't smell any telltale sign of alcohol on her breath. "I'm just tired of denying what I want."

"And what's that?" There would be no question in either of their minds she'd given consent.

"I want you to spank me and then fuck me." She leaned forward and nibbled at his neck. "Fuck me hard like you mean it."

With those words, he knew he couldn't be gentle. He didn't question her again, rather he took hold of her and bent her so her upper body was across the vanity with her backside in the air. In one swift move, he had her skirt up and her panties down around her ankles.

He gave her no warning before raising his hand and bringing it down hard across her ass. She yelped, and he did it again. "Is this what you want?" he asked. "My hand turning your backside red, punishing you for thinking another man could give what you need?"

She nodded, but he shook his head. "I need more than a nod tonight, Lilly. Let me hear the words. I need you to say them."

"Yes, damn it," she said.

He gave her another hard swat. "Are you cursing at me? You're going to make me wish I'd brought my belt."

"Fuck you."

"Now. Now," he said. "Who's the only one getting fucked tonight?"

She glared at him and he grinned. He'd rarely seen her act this petulant before. That she was acting so out of character only seemed to prove to him how much she needed this. He wasn't sure how long it'd been since she'd played with anyone, but he remembered from their time together how she needed the regular release of a hard spanking. If he'd had even the slightest inkling that this would end up happening, he'd had definitely brought his belt. A hard hand spanking was nice, and it served its purpose, but when it'd been too long between sessions, she craved his belt.

Since he didn't have one with him, he'd have to improvise this round, going harder and longer. She melted under his hands and for a few minutes, it was as if they'd never been apart.

Because they'd been together for so long before the divorce, he'd once known her body almost better than he knew his own. It pleased him to discover all that knowledge came back as soon as he touched her. He wanted to take her to her edge, but again, he wasn't sure how long it'd been since she'd played. It'd be better this time not to get her quite as deep as she'd like, just to make sure he didn't take her too far.

As expected, when he went to pull her skirt down, a symbol he'd finished, she protested. He took a firm hold of her wrist. "Don't forget who's in charge here. If you want me to continue, you need to accept it when I say you've had enough."

Though he'd spanked her in the bathroom, he'd reigned in his control enough to ensure they at least made it to the bed before continuing. But once there, she looked at him and said, "I almost agreed to play with Eric tonight," and he felt his control slip away.

"What do you mean by almost?" he growled out.

She was on her back in the middle of the bed. After placing her there, Ty had returned to the floor. But when she'd uttered that sentence in her casual, just-so-you-know tone, he'd moved back on top. Now he had her underneath him and his hands on either side of her head.

"Tell me," he said.

"We went for a walk after dinner. It had been such a good night. When we finished walking, he asked me if I'd like to play once we both returned home." She took a deep breath. "I could come up with two hundred reasons to say yes, and as hard as I tried, I only had one to say no."

And yet, based on what she'd said moments prior, that had been her answer.

"But that one reason to say no was greater than the two hundred ones to say yes." She lifted her hand to cup the side of his face. "I said no because he wasn't you."

n

CHAPTER 15
LILLIAN

Lillian held her breath, waiting for Ty's response. She half expected him to jump off the bed and run outside to find Eric in order to beat him up. Or she thought he might say something sarcastic or, perhaps, gloat. What she was not expecting was he did.

"Lillian," he whispered, lowering his head. "I've missed you so." He finished in the instant before their lips touched in a brief kiss.

Yes, she wanted to shout as his lips came again, more insistent than before. His kiss was a reclaiming, and she knew it'd been foolish of her to think that anyone could ever replace him in her life. At the moment, she didn't know what that meant or what it looked like, and for once she didn't care. For once, she was going to take what she wanted, and tonight she wanted Ty.

She ran her hands up his arms and then slid them down his back. His body was both familiar and foreign at the same time. He pulled away to undress, and she whimpered even though it only took him seconds. She'd lost her dress somewhere between the bathroom and the bedroom. It was unclear which one of them had taken it off of her.

Ty situated himself over her again, this time settling himself between her legs. He kissed her briefly before trailing his lips downward, tasting every inch of her it seemed. Her back arched when he surprised her by covering a nipple with his mouth and giving a hard suck.

Fuck. The sharp, exquisite pain, such a beautiful contrast to the gentle way he'd been touching the rest of her body. He repeated the action on the other side and she moaned in pleasure. She hadn't remembered it feeling this good, but how was it possible now would be better?

He moved lower, his lips brushing her belly, and she stopped trying to explain how and surrendered to feeling the now.

"How is it possible you taste better than I remember?" he murmured against her skin, his question echoing her own.

He went lower, blowing warm air across her heated and needy flesh, sending a shiver of pleasure through her. She bit the inside of her cheek when his fingertip followed and he gave a low chuckle, finding her so wet.

"Which one aroused you more?" he asked. "The spanking I gave you, or having my mouth on you?"

There was no way she could decide between the two of them, so she replied, "They were both equally arousing. Just in different ways."

He laughed against the skin of her inner thigh. "I always said your talent was wasted on me and Isaac. You should be in law."

It was a strange thing to comment on in the middle of sex. Saying nothing else, he shifted his body, slipping his arms underneath her hips and bringing her to his mouth. She let a groan escape from her throat when his tongue circled her clit, slipped inside her, back out, and circled again.

"Don't come yet," he said, which she thought was horribly unfair seeing as how she hadn't had sex in almost three years.

"Not sure I can stop it from happening, " she confessed.

"You better," he said. "If you come before I give you permission, I won't fuck you. Instead, you can watch as I get myself off. Leaving you to only imagine how it would have felt to have my thick, hard dick fucking your greedy pussy."

"Ass," she said, because that's what he was being, even though she secretly loved it as well as the fact he still wanted to command her.

"You want me to fuck your ass instead?" He lowered her hips back to the bed. "Because that can be arranged. Maybe not the first time, though."

He was verbally teasing her during sex. She was certain he'd done so before, but at the moment she couldn't remember any specific instance of him doing so. It relaxed her, making her feel more comfortable. There was something altogether sexy about a man who wasn't afraid to make his partner laugh in bed. Although she had to admit, in Ty's case, it helped that he was built like a sex god.

"I'll have to take a rain check for the dick up my ass," she teased back. "Not that I'm opposed to anal sex, but I'm not sure I'm adequately prepared for that task at the moment." She would never turn down anal sex. It had always been one of her favorites with Ty, but that had been years ago.

"That's fine with me," Ty said. Though they had been talking, his hands had never stopped, keeping her body hot and aroused. "I don't think either one of us will be bored tonight."

He pulled away from her, probably because he wanted her to get into another position, and couldn't resist a look at his cock. He was hard and ready for her. Just a glance at his length left her feeling desperate to be filled.

Of course, he caught her looking and reached down to give himself a stroke. "Think you're ready to take it?"

"Yes. Now. Please."

He didn't budge. "You can do better."

"I said please." What she really wanted to do was take him in her mouth. Feel him fuck the back of her throat. But she wasn't the only one on edge. She knew from the way his muscles strained that it was a precarious position for him to be in. If she put her mouth on him, he probably wouldn't last very long.

He hadn't replied to her statement. She tore her gaze from his crotch and looked up to meet his eyes. He lifted one eyebrow.

Damn. She was an idiot. "Yes. Now. Please. Sir."

The corner of his mouth quirked up. "Hands and knees."

She took her time getting into position and wiggled her ass while she got situated.

"Feeling a bit cheeky?" He gave the already reddened skin a hard swat, and she swallowed her moan. "I've changed my mind. I want you on your back. Every thrust of my cock will be a reminder of the spanking I gave you. The faster and harder I fuck you, the more your ass will hurt. Get ready, I'm going to ride you hard."

"Yes, Sir," she said, surprised she could speak at all because, damn, she'd been celibate for the last few years, and wasn't sure her body could withstand much more of him talking without touching her.

"Move it, then. Faster." He jerked his cock as she scrambled to get into position. "Fuck. I've never been so hard. Are you sure you can handle this?"

She looked between her legs at him. Holy hell, she didn't remember him being that long and thick. But she wanted him to fill her and to do it so completely there was no room for anything else. "Yes, Sir, and don't be gentle."

He didn't reply, but lined himself up with only the tip inside her. It wasn't nearly enough, and she whined. Before the whine finished, he grabbed her legs, one in each hand and thrust into her with one hard push.

For a handful of seconds, she couldn't breathe, and she was positive she saw stars. All it took was the one thrust and her orgasm crashed over her. Ty continued pounding into her, again and again, even as her body shook with a second climax.

"Ty!" She shouted. "Fuck. Yes."

He gave one last thrust and she felt him release inside her.

"Oh my, God," she panted, as he rolled over and brought her to rest on top of him. "I may never move again."

"Did I hurt you?" He was as breathless as she was, but she still heard the concern in his voice.

"Hell, no," she said. "I meant move out of this bed. You do plan on doing that again, right?"

Long after Ty's breathing fell into the steady cadence of sleep, Lillian found herself unable to follow him. It wasn't regret that kept her awake. Not at all. She didn't regret one thing that had happened between her and Ty just now. In fact, she was glad that it happened.

Ever since the divorce, she'd feared something was wrong with her and that she'd never experience desire and need the way she had with Ty. Now she knew she could. That it'd been with Ty wasn't much of a surprise. Part of her had always known how impossible he'd be to walk away from.

With that realization, she had to ask herself the hard questions she'd been avoiding. Could she play with anyone other than Ty? She didn't think so, now more than ever.

But she's wouldn't allow herself to dwell on that topic or to view it as a problem. No, why should she view it as a problem? She'd accepted the fact she still loved him weeks ago.

Her issues stemmed from the knowledge that she would never be able to trust him completely again. Without trust, there was no marriage. Without trust, they couldn't even run the simplest of kink scenarios.

She knew what she had to do, she only hoped she could go through with it when the time came. Not right this second, though. No, she could rest in the comfort of his arms for a few more minutes.

CHAPTER 16
TY

Ty knew something wasn't right the second he woke up. For one, he was in a bed and not waking up on the floor, but it was more than that. With his eyes still closed, he turned toward the spot Lillian should be and reached for her warmth.

His hands grasped nothing. Her side of the bed was empty, but not only that, it carried not a bit of heat. She was gone and had been for quite some time.

The realization startled him, and he woke completely, sitting straight up in the bed. Lillian wasn't anywhere in the room. Without moving, he took in the open closet which now only held his clothes. He didn't need to check the bathroom to know it would be just as empty. She'd left him.

Not only had she left him, she'd sneaked out in the dead of night, without saying goodbye, and after some of the best sex he'd ever had. What the fuck?

A glance at his phone told him it was only six thirty. How long ago had she left? He jumped out of bed and threw on the clothes he'd thrown on the floor the night before. Of course, the car keys for the ridiculous rental car were also gone. Damn, he hated the thought of her on the road and driving that matchbook of a car.

He didn't have to think about where he was going. Moving with purpose, he wasted no time in making his way to the main building. As expected, Eric was already there with coffee. Ty didn't even want a cup this morning. Ignoring everything else, he strode across the floor to stand in front of Eric.

"Ty," Eric said with a nod, like everything was fine.

"What the hell happened with you and Lillian last night?"

"We had a pleasant dinner and took a walk." He shrugged. "Then I brought her back here. I'm surprised she didn't tell you the same. Why are you asking me?"

"Because she left this morning." Ty realized his mistake as soon as the words left his mouth. In wanting to know why Lillian left, he needed to blame someone, and he picked Eric without thought. But the truth was, if anyone was to blame, it was Ty himself.

Eric realized the same thing almost immediately. He narrowed his eyes at Ty. "She left this morning? Maybe I should ask you what the hell happened last night?"

Ty didn't respond, which only made Eric study him closer. Ty held his ground, refusing to give Eric an ounce of satisfaction by fidgeting like a boy caught with his hands in the cookie jar.

"I'd be right in asking that question, too, I believe." Eric pointed at Ty's neck. "Are those scratch marks? I don't remember seeing them yesterday."

Ty turned to make his way back to the cabin. He'd go back and try to call her. If he'd had a thought in his head, he'd have done that very thing before trying to go after Eric. Damn it. He'd been so sure it was the other man. And it wasn't. It was him. She'd left because they'd slept together last night.

"Hold up." Eric put a hand on his shoulder. "You're not walking away from me that fast. Why don't you tell me the real reason Lillian left today?"

"I don't know," Ty said. "I'm going to get my phone and call her."

Eric didn't remove his hand. "Do you want to know what happened with me and Lillian last night? I'll tell you."

Ty turned to face him. "Go on."

"We had dinner at a nice seafood restaurant, and I don't think it's disingenuous for me to say we both had an enjoyable time. I, for one, wasn't ready for the night to be over and I didn't think she was either. I gave her the choice of coming back here or going on a walk."

"That's pretty much what she told me."

Eric gave no indication that he'd spoken. "We walked along the beach for some time, just chatting, nothing major, just getting to know each other stuff. On our way back here, I told her I'd enjoyed her company and would like to get the chance to get to know her better when we were both back home. I also told her I'd like for us to visit The Club together, if she'd feel comfortable with that."

Ty took a deep breath to make himself calm down. Eric and Lillian had done nothing other than dinner, a walk, and a pleasant chat.

"I really thought she'd agree." Eric shrugged. "But she told me she'd enjoyed our meal, and while she was glad she got to know me better, she didn't envision herself playing with anyone. Possibly ever."

Ty held his breath at his words. Possibly ever.

"I don't know how, but somehow you still have a hold on her," Eric said. "I also know that you don't give a fuck about what I think, but I'm going to tell you, anyway. Lillian is an exceptional woman. You know this, of course, because you were smart enough to marry her. What you may not know or fully comprehend is how exceptional she has remained after your divorce."

Of course he knew that as well, he wanted to tell the man. Ty also wanted to add that he didn't appreciate his tone and the way he kept insinuating that he somehow knew Lillian better than Ty did.

"But when she turned me down last night, I realized something I don't think you're aware of, even after whatever happened between the two of you last night."

"And what is that?" Ty asked.

"Behind her facade of a strong, independent, single woman is a lost and lonely submissive who desperately needs her Master. Either find a way to be that for her, or help her find someone who can."

CHAPTER 17
LILLIAN

Lillian left the resort at five thirty in the morning. Even though she knew Celeste was awake, she waited until she'd found a coffee shop on the mainland four hours later before calling her London friend. If she called any sooner, she feared Celeste would think there was an emergency, and Lillian didn't want to worry her.

The two women had grown close over the last several months. It was hard for Lillian to believe that Lance would have ever settled down. Of the three friends, he was the one everyone thought of as Most Likely to Remain a Bachelor Forever. Not that anyone considered him a player. He wasn't. Yet it was safe to say he'd always enjoyed playing with a variety of women.

All that changed the day he offered to take over the audition process for his family's scholarship to Juilliard since his grandmother was in the hospital.

"Lillian?" Celeste answered with. "How are you? Aren't you still in Florida?"

Just hearing her friend's voice coming through the phone was enough to make her warm inside.

"I'm still in Florida, but I'm not with Restoration any more." That was the first thing she did upon arriving at the coffee shop moments earlier was to call their main number and let them know she was leaving because of family complications.

"What happened?" Celeste asked.

Lillian told he the entire story, starting with her stupid idea to go to The Club right up until this morning when she left. The entire time, Celeste was silent, letting Lillian do all the talking.

"Oh, girl," Celeste finally said once Lillian told her everything. "You're in a mess and a half."

"Tell me about it." Lillian ran her fingers through her hair. She hadn't taken a shower this morning because she wanted to leave without waking Ty. She was almost certain she could smell him on her skin. "I don't know what to do at this point."

"Then don't do anything," Celeste said, as if it made all the sense in the world.

"What?"

"Take it from me," her friend said. "Someone who had to learn this lesson the hard way. Don't do anything. Where are you now?"

"Just outside of Miami."

"Excellent. Here's what you do. Book yourself a suite at a five-star hotel. You're not due anywhere for the next week and a half. Spend a few days investing in you. Go to the spa. Read a book. Rest."

The idea of even one day to just relax boggled her mind, much less more than one. "I can't in good consciousness spend days lounging around a spa when I'm supposed to be rebuilding a home for a family left homeless by two hurricanes."

"Normally, I would agree with you, but in this case, I would argue you tried to do that very thing, and you would still be doing it if your ex-husband and the project's team lead hadn't gotten into a contest trying to figure out who had the biggest dick."

Lillian smiled and gave a little laugh at the picture Celeste's words brought to mind.

"See?" Celeste asked. "You know I'm right." Before Lillian could comment on anything, Celeste asked, "You said you're in Miami, right?"

"Yes, why?"

"I have my laptop right here, and I'm looking to see who has vacancy. I wouldn't think it's currently Miami's high season, but then again, what do I know?" The sound of typing came through the phone. "Here we go. The Faena has availability. That's a nice one. Yup, this is where you need to go chill out for a few days. I'm going to send you this link. Oh, look at that, they have a suite available. Call and book it. Don't make me fly across the ocean, because you know I will."

Lillian could only laugh, because she knew Celeste meant every word. "I'll call them as soon as I hang up with you."

"That's more like it. That's what I want to hear."

"How's London?" Lillian asked. "Still treating you and Lance well?"

"No complaints here," Celeste said. "The group is playing in Austria next weekend. Lance and I are sneaking away a few days early, so we can explore a bit."

Celeste was a world class violinist who played for a European touring orchestra based in London. Lillian still shook her head when she imagined Lance, over ten years older than the love of his life, following her around like a lovesick groupie.

"Be sure to keep that man of yours in check," Lillian said. "I've worked with him, I know how sneaky he can be."

Celeste snored. "Nah, you just have to learn how to play him."

"Well," Lillian said. "Between the two of us, you're the one with the most experience in learning how to play hard things." At the giggles Celeste made, Lillian realized what she'd said. "I mean, you know how to play with hard things."

But that only made Celeste break into laughter.

"Damn it," Lillian said. "You know what I mean."

"I do," Celeste said, trying to catch her breath. "But it's so much fun listening to you make unintentional dirty innuendos."

"Whatever." Lillian rolled her eyes. "I'm going to call that hotel. Goodbye."

****

Celeste was still giggling after saying goodbye to Lillian.

"Sounds like a fun conversation."

She turned her head to find Lance standing in the doorway, leaning against the frame, watching her with amusement dancing in his eyes. It never failed to take her breath away that he was hers. How did she get so lucky? Sometimes she had to pinch herself because surely she was dreaming. How was it possible he'd followed her across the ocean? Then after he found her, he stayed and uprooted his entire life to stay because her dream job was here and he didn't want to be without her?

She stood up and made her way over to him. From all appearances, he'd finished work early. When he first told her he'd be cutting back his hours, she'd been skeptical, not understanding how he could do anything of the sort while working in an international office. But he'd done it.

She ran her hand across his chest. "Finished with work?"

He gave her a slow grin and tugged her closer. "For the day. Do you have practice?"

"No, I did it earlier." She closed her eyes in bliss as he pulled the pin out of her hair, setting her long waves free to fall past her shoulders. "That was Lillian on the phone."

He'd been leaning down, probably preparing to kiss her, but held still at her words. "Was it? I thought she was doing some volunteer work down in the Keys?"

"She was, but." Damn it. She didn't want to talk about Lillian. Not with Lance standing so close, and especially since he had the look in his eye that told her he had very naughty things planned.

"Long story short, she's in Miami because Ty is a dick," she said. "I know he's your friend and business partner, but that doesn't exempt him from dickness."

Lance chuckled. "I'd have to agree with you on that. Ty never has been able to think straight around Lillian. I'd hoped with both of them being in New York they'd finally be able to work things out."

"Don't give up all hope just yet," she said. "I told her to stop running for a few days and chill in Miami."

Lance nodded. "Where's she staying?"

"I found her a suite at the Faena. Not sure that's where she'll end up, but it looked like her."

He ran his thumb over her bottom lip. "Did you tell her our news?"

Celeste palmed her left hand up against his chest, enabling her to better see the ring he'd proposed with two days ago. "No," she said. "It didn't feel right to share my news when she called me as upset as she was. I thought it'd be better for me to keep it to myself for now and tell her when she's in a better mood."

"You're probably right," he said. "I doubt I'd tell Ty if he were to call me just now. It'd be too much like rubbing salt into a wound."

"Exactly." She tilted her head up in order to see him better. This man, her fiancé, who would soon become her husband. It made her feel giddy, a word she rarely used and had never applied to herself before. "Since we can't celebrate with our friends, and we're both free, I suggest we have our own private celebration. Naked."

"Again?" he said. "Are you sure you're up to another celebration?"

"I'm not the one who needs to be up," she egged him on. "I think that depends entirely on you. But if you feel like you can't, you know, be up for another celebration — "

He placed a finger over her lips. "You better stop while you're ahead, little girl, or you're going to see up close and personal how up I am."

She tucked he fingers into the waistband of his pants. "I'm counting on it."

CHAPTER 18
TY

Twenty-four hours later, Ty still didn't know where Lillian was, much less how she was doing. To say he was on the edge was to put it mildly. She had returned none of the messages he left for her or replied to a single one of the many texts he'd sent. Would it really take that much effort on her part to at least send something, so he'd know she was okay? He'd welcome anything. Even a text that simply said, "I'm fine, you asshole. Leave me alone."

For a moment or two he contemplated going after her, but he knew how much work the volunteers had left to do. It would be difficult enough for them to get everything done while down one person. He couldn't in good conscious leave them down two.

He called and spoke with Isaac, but his business partner hadn't heard from Lillian. Nor did he seem to be overly concerned about her whereabouts.

"Lillian is a grown woman, who is ridiculously intelligent and has been living on her own, perfectly fine I might add, without you babysitting her for a good number of years." Isaac's tone implied he wouldn't listen to anything Ty said. Secretly, he couldn't help but wonder if Lillian might have called her old boss to update him on the situation and to let him know she was doing.

Ty had called the airports, but of course, no one would give him any information because of privacy laws. Yes, he should be glad, and truthfully, he was, but couldn't someone let it slip if she'd left the country or not?

"You really wouldn't want them to do that, would you?" Eric asked him forty-eight hours after she'd left. "I mean, if they slip and give the information to you, who's to say they won't slip and give it to anyone who calls and asks?"

Ty knew Eric spoke the truth, but couldn't the guy at least agree with him a little? It was six-thirty in the evening, and they had just arrived back at the resort. Since Lillian had taken the rental with her, Ty had ridden in the van with Eric to and from the job site for the last few days.

"I know you're right," Ty told Eric in response to his question. "I just want to know she's okay and to hear if from her mouth." He wanted a lot more than that, but he wouldn't admit as much to Eric, even though he was certain the man already knew.

Eric said nothing in response, rather he slapped him on the shoulder. "Good work today, man. See you in a few for dinner."

Ty nodded, and they went their separate ways. He wasn't hungry and didn't feel like eating or sitting around and talking with everyone. However, experience had taught him that if he didn't eat now, with all the manual labor he'd put in today, he'd be ravenous at midnight and unable to sleep. Dinner wouldn't start until seven, so he had time to take a shower and place more messages to Lillian before then.

He'd just stepped inside the empty cabin when his phone rang. Heart pounding, he pulled it from his pocket. Lillian. At last.

His heart sank for a minute when he realized it wasn't her, but curiosity got the best of him, and he answered because why the hell was Lance calling him at this time of night?

"Lance?" he asked. "Is everything alright? It's not Celeste, is it?" Ty couldn't think of another reason he'd be calling from London so late. Wasn't it almost midnight? He hoped nothing was wrong with Celeste. Ty had only met her a few times, but he could only imagine how devastated Lance would be if anything happened to her.

"No," Lance said. "She's fine. Right here beside me, actually."

Ty's mind raced. Lance sounded too calm for it to be anything bad. That meant his call probably had nothing to do with his grandmother, Barbara, being ill, either. "What's up?"

"First of all," Lance started. "Celeste and I have been discussing whether we should even be having this call."

"Okay," he said, not understanding at all where the man was going.

"I'm not sure if you're aware, but Celeste and Lillian have become friends," he said, and no, Ty had not known that little tidbit. "Anyway, Lillian called her yesterday morning—"

"She did?" He found he couldn't stop himself from asking. "How is she? Is she okay? Where is she?"

Lance sighed. "See? This is why I wasn't going to call you, but Celeste thinks differently, and I'm learning she's usually right."

"What do you mean you weren't going to call me?"

"Because I didn't want you taking off half-ass, and without thinking."

Ty was getting ready to say he never did half-ass things without thinking, but then he looked around the cabin he was currently having the conversation in and thought better of it. He took a deep breath. "I'm calm. I can handle it."

"Lillian's in Miami," Lance said. "Staying at The Faena. I'm telling you this because you and Lillian have some things to work out. I don't know if working them out will get you back together, but I think you'll both be a lot more… content, and at least be able to move on."

Ty didn't tell him he didn't want to be content or to move on if it meant doing so without Lillian.

"What I think you should do," Lance said. "What I'm asking you to do is to spend time tonight thinking about what you need to say to her, and only then go to see her."

Two thousand questions ran through his head. "How do I know she'll still be there? How long is she staying? Does Celeste know?"

"Yes," Lance said, and damn it, if his calm attitude wasn't obnoxious. Ty wanted to remind him what a fit he'd been in when Celeste ran off without a word, and Ty just happened to see her at a concert he attended with his sister. But he kept silent. "Celeste talked with her earlier today, and Lillian indicated she'd be staying through the weekend and not leaving until Sunday or Monday at the earliest."

Ty breathed a sigh of relief. That gave him plenty of time to think and plan. "Thank you."

IT WAS WELL after two o'clock in the morning before Ty could close his eyes and get some sleep. He'd followed Lance's advice to spend the evening in thought. After ending the phone call, he picked up dinner from the main building and took it back to the cabin, needing the privacy to think and plan.

His path forward was clear along with the steps he needed to take while on that path. Surprisingly enough, what he needed to do wasn't what kept him up until the early hours of the morning. He figured that part out quickly. It was how he was going to do what he needed to be done.

CHAPTER 19
LILLIAN

It didn't take long for Lillian to decide she could get used to being pampered. She wasn't sure how Celeste knew about this particular hotel, if she'd been a guest herself, or if she'd only known of it by reputation. But for whatever reason it was, Lillian was immensely grateful.

After getting up before dawn in order to avoid Ty and driving back to Miami in the turnip car, when she finally stepped into the lobby, she was exhausted. She'd made her reservation on-line after getting off the phone with Celeste and knew she must have looked questionable walking up to the front desk to check in. Even if the woman working the desk didn't look put off by her appearance, Lillian felt out of place. Of course, that might have been the irrational fear she smelled like sex.

Not that anyone said anything of the sort to her. Within minutes of arriving, she was standing in the middle of a suite with the one carryon bag she'd packed for two weeks. Though she feared her skin still smelled of sex, she couldn't find the energy to drag herself to the spa-like shower waiting in the bathroom. Instead, she stripped down naked and climbed into the inviting bed. She was asleep within seconds.

She couldn't recall the last time she'd taken a nap, and when she woke up later in the afternoon, she felt revived and decadent. After a leisurely shower, she ordered a late lunch/early dinner from the room service menu and ate while wrapped up in one of the hotel's fluffy bathrobes. It would have been an all-around wonderful day except for one thing.

Ty.

She realized now there was no way she could pretend as if he didn't exist. Not with both of them in the same city. If she were honest with herself, she had to admit she didn't want to pretend as if he didn't exist. As the day slipped away into night, she allowed herself to imagine what it would look like if she let him back into her life.

Late in the morning the next day, she still wasn't sure. She was making her way back to her room following a morning at the hotel's spa. Her current plan for the rest of the day was lunch by the pool and a few hours reading the book she'd downloaded to her phone after overhearing it discussed by several ladies at the spa.

She stepped out of the elevator, faltering when she saw him standing at her door. Damn. How had he found her so quickly?

"Ty," she said, like she'd been expecting him. "At least you're outside my room this time. Better security than the last place I stayed."

He gave a half smile. "Yeah, but to be honest, I didn't try to get inside this time."

"Progress, I suppose," she said. "But I have to say I'm surprised they gave you my room number." She made a mental note to chat with hotel management before leaving to give them her opinion on their shortcomings regarding guest privacy and the resulting potential security issues.

"I didn't get the room number from them."

She turned around from where she'd been unlocking the door. "You didn't? Then who did you get it from?"

"Lance."

Ah, that explained it. She went back to unlocking the door and waved him inside once she opened it. Might as well, he was already here, and if she didn't let him in to say whatever it was he needed to get off his chest, he would keep popping up until she listened to him.

That was the lie she told herself. Inside she was doing cartwheels he'd tracked her down and was now in her suite.

"I should apologize for running off the way I did yesterday," she said, walking into the living room. At his silence, she turned around to make sure he'd followed her. He had, but what was that look on his face? And why was he not saying anything? It wasn't like him at all, and it was freaking her out a bit. "Ty?"

At his name, he shook his head. "I can't do this."

"Do what?"

He didn't reply, but crossed the floor to where she stood and before she could comprehend what he was doing, he'd taken her in his arms and was kissing her. It was so unexpected, so unlike him, and so....

Everything.

She responded without hesitation, putting her arms around him, pulling him close. Something inside her needed to feel his desire for her, needed to know how she made him feel. Ludicrous, really. Especially considering how thoroughly he'd taken her not all that long ago.

It was at that moment, there in his arms, that everything she'd been questioning for the last twenty-four hours, or last two years to be more accurate, fell into place and made sense. Ty was it for her. There was nothing she could do to change anything.

She couldn't understand, but something told her she could trust him. Not that what he'd done was in any way right or okay, she would never believe there was an excuse for cheating. But somehow she knew everything would turn out to be okay. Maybe the hypnosis session would prove to be of benefit.

At the moment, though, all she wanted to think about or focus on was him. The urgency in him was unexpected, and she didn't understand why he acted as if they were running against time.

"Are you due back to the volunteer center?" She pulled back to ask.

"I'm going back," he said. "But not right now."

"Is that why you came here? To take me back to finish? Because I can't.... I..."

"No, that's not it," he said, his lips nibbled and teased the skin of her neck. "But I don't want to talk right now. Just give me this. Just give us this."

It wasn't smart. They really needed to talk before they fell into bed again. On some level she knew all she was doing was opening her heart up to more pain. At the moment, however, she didn't care. With her recent revelation about her relationship with Ty, the only thing she wanted was him.

She reached down and took his hand. "Come with me."

She didn't tell him where they were headed. She didn't need to.

They only took a few steps into the bedroom before they came to a stop. Lillian reached for Ty's shirt tail and pulled it up, needing to feel him, to prove to herself he was real.

"Take it off." He pulled at the casual outfit she'd worn to the spa, obviously feeling the same urges she had. "I need to see you."

She couldn't agree more. Days ago, the cabin had been too dark for her to see as much of him as she'd have liked. Her fingers trembled as she worked to undress, and she couldn't figure out why. There was no way she was fearful.

They'd been together for far too long for her to fear anything he might ask of her.

"Are you cold?" He must have picked up on her trembling.

"I don't think so. I'm not sure what my problem is. Probably excitement."

"I don't remember making you tremble before." He was already naked and standing by the bed. "Come here and let me hold you."

She walked to him without hesitation. He smiled as he put his arms around her, gathering her in his embrace. "I didn't think it was fear of me."

Never. "I never fear when I'm around you."

"Good," he said, and went to work undressing her. As he took each item of clothing off, he kissed the skin he revealed. She shivered when his lips brushed her shoulder. He gave a little chuckle, and when he spoke again it was with the low tone that always curled her toes. "Yes. That's the reaction I'm looking for."

He continued his task, tracing her curves with his fingers. Under his touch, her skin came alive and need burned throughout her body. Her knees weakened, and she shifted her feet to steady her stance. A move that did not go unnoticed by Ty.

"Hold on to me, Lillian," he said, his mouth teasing the skin of her belly, as he eased her shorts down and over her hips. "I won't let you fall."

She placed her hands on his shoulders, relishing the feel of his muscles under her fingertips. Such broad shoulders. Broad enough to carry both her and her burdens, surely. If she'd allow him the opportunity.

He picked her up and gently placed her on the bed. Unlike their last joining, however, he moved as if he had all the time in the world. Maybe they did. With each leisurely stroke of his fingers over her skin, he awoke sensations long forgotten. She reached for him, wanting to do the same to him, but he shook his head. Never, in all the times they'd been together in years past, had he ever made love to her so tenderly.

His tasted and touched her, and at times it seemed he did so not as if he was trying to remember, but rather ensuring he didn't forgot. But that didn't make any sense. All she could do was hold onto him, enjoying the pleasure his worshipful loving brought her.

Even when he finally entered her, it was slow and sensual. At times, he almost stopped, holding still, leaving his imprint inside her.

"Lillian," he whispered when at last he brought them both to release, his tone almost mournful.

All at once, she realized what he was doing.

He was saying goodbye.

CHAPTER 20
TY

He wouldn't have thought it possible, but Ty believed he hated himself more for resting in Lillian's opulent suite than he did the day of their divorce. His plan had been to come to Miami and talk with her. To put everything on the table and to be completely honest. He'd tell her about how he thought late into the night and into the early morning hours. How he'd come to understand the best things he could give her were space and freedom. It was unfair of him to hold her back from getting on with her life. She deserved to be loved by a man worthy of her. To serve a Dom worthy of her service.

That had been the plan.

But that plan had been shot straight to hell the second she stepped off the elevator. How could he let her go again? How could he turn around and leave without her beside him? He remembered all too well the depression he went through when he first moved to London. But that was a selfish reason, and he couldn't justify denying her happiness just so he wouldn't be depressed.

Then she tried to apologize for leaving the Restoration group. Like the entire situation was somehow her fault, even though he was the asshole who followed her to Florida in the first place. He couldn't believe it crossed her mind to apologize. Yet, there she'd stood in the hall, the only woman he'd ever wanted. The only woman he would ever want. It wasn't until his lips were on hers that he knew what he was doing. He wanted to love her one more time.

He thought he'd covered his emotions, buried them deep down inside himself, along with the reason for why he was doing what he was. But now he wasn't so certain. Not with Lillian in his arms, looking at him with too many questions in her eyes.

"You're leaving, aren't you?" Lillian asked.

"Not right this second."

"But soon," she said. "I didn't realize until just now, but you didn't bring a suitcase. You're going back to Restoration."

"I need to help them finish," he said simply, but that wasn't the only reason or even the main one.

"That makes me feel like I should go back."

He shook his head. "No one expects that."

"But — "

He stopped her. "It's my fault. I shouldn't have followed you in the first place." Looking back at it, that's what he'd done. Followed her like he was a stalker or something. If some other man had followed her, that's what Ty would have called him, a stalker. "And we both know it."

"But you did, and that—"

"Changed nothing."

"But it did."

Damn, he wanted that to be the case. But it couldn't be, no matter how badly he wanted things to have changed between them. They hadn't, and they never would.

She pushed up on her elbows from where she'd been resting with her head on his chest and loomed over him. Her eyes glistened with unshed tears. Fuck. He hated it when she cried. He hated it even more when he was the cause of her tears. He told himself this would be the last time, but it didn't make him feel any better.

"Lillian," he said. "You deserve more than me. You deserve a man who will give you the moon on a silver platter. One you can trust implicitly and without the drama and baggage that comes with me. And you need a Dom you know will always have your needs and best interest at heart."

She remained silent, shaking her head as a tear ran down the slope of cheek. "No," she finally whispered. "All I need is you."

"You don't need me. Hell, the last few years have proven that. I'm comfortable, is all," Ty said. "Like an old tattered blanket. And I'm the only Dom you've ever served. You deserve more and you should demand it."

He took a deep breath and made himself continue, to say the words he had to. "Eric really likes you, and you know yourself how much he wants to see you when you're both home. And, as much as it pains me to say, he's a really great guy, and based on the information I've gathered, a top notch Dominant. He can give you the things I can't."

"That's why you're leaving me today?" she asked. "Because you think once you're gone, I'm going to fall madly in love with Eric when he flies back home?"

"No," he said, trying to lighten the mood. "I'm well aware it won't happen instantaneously, it'll probably take a day or two."

"This isn't funny."

"I never said it was." Because she was one hundred and ten percent right, there wasn't anything about their current situation funny. "You need to experience more than what I can offer, and you can't do it with me always underfoot."

"How dare you stand there and try to tell me what I need? You don't have a clue as to what I need. And news flash, you were across the ocean for over two years, and I still couldn't move on with another Dom. It has nothing to do with you being underfoot."

He sighed. This was not going well. He pulled them both up so they were sitting in bed, and she tucked the sheet around her.

"Do you remember the conversation we had the morning of our first day? When we were driving to the job site?" He waited for her nod before he continued. "You asked why we never went back to Charleston, and I said it was because we knew going back wouldn't be the same. Don't you see, we're the exact same way. What we were before is like Charleston, and just like going back for a visit today wouldn't be the same as the first time. You and I can't go back to who we were. I told you that day, if we went back to Charleston, we'd tarnish its memory with our current reality. If we tried to go back to who we were, it would do the same. I can remember the good times we had then, Lillian, I don't want to tarnish them."

But if he'd thought he'd be able to talk any sense into her, the vehement way she shook her head would have clued him into her unwillingness to listen to reason.

"Why the hell would I want to go back to who we were?" she asked him. "I happen to like the person the last few years have shaped me into. Most of the time, anyway. I'm a lot more independent now. I'm more sure of my abilities and strengths. I don't want to go back to the old me. And so what if Charleston looks different when we returned? It's supposed to, that's what time does, it changes things. But those changes aren't bad, they only give us more to learn. So, of course, you and I won't be the same way we were. It's impossible. We're different, and we'll be different together, but different isn't bad. It just means we have to relearn each other."

She wasn't going to change her mind, and he knew he had to get away. Knew that if he didn't, she'd break his resolve to do the right thing. "I can't, Lillian," he said. "I'm sorry, I just can't."

CHAPTER 21
LILLIAN

Lillian didn't tell anyone she was back in Manhattan. If she told anyone, they'd want to know why she was back early, forcing her to make something up, because she couldn't tell them the truth. Not to mention, whenever she thought about the reasons she left, she'd tear up. And she couldn't have that because then she'd have to make up a reason she was crying.

Bottom line? She didn't want anyone knowing she'd all but thrown herself at her ex-husband, and he'd rejected her. There was little she could imagine that would be more humiliating. And, in case that wasn't bad enough, after she told them everything, they'd look at her with pity. She'd gone through months of being on the receiving end of that look during and after the divorce. She had no desire to repeat the experience.

The guilty feeling she had about leaving Restoration followed her home. She'd kept in contact with Eric via text, and he told her they were fine. Of course they missed her and were sorry she had to leave, but they were on track to finish the house on time. She wondered what reason they gave to everyone about her departure and then decided it was better not to know. She never asked Eric about Ty, and he never brought up his name.

To keep herself busy and her mind occupied, she organized her apartment. A task she could never quite work up enough effort to tackle when she was working over sixty hours a week for Isaac.

Now, she had days of nothing planned, and she refused to waste one minute of one day thinking about Ty. It didn't work that way, of course. It never did. So while she couldn't banish him from her mind, at least she could keep him on the fringes.

She methodically went through her closet, sorting every piece of clothing into one of three piles, keep, give away, and for the unsalvageable items, trash. When she finished, she organized the keep items in the closet by type, and then by color. She blamed the color thing on Isaac and made a note to smack him the next time she saw him.

There was a women's shelter not too far from the building Ty and the others worked. She'd read a newspaper article about it on the flight back from Miami. Not only did they provide a safe place for women and children, but they also worked with the women on job skills. There had been a request for gently used business attire that could be given to the women.

When she'd read the request, her mind took her back to the day she was packing for Florida. How many business suits did she have that she rarely wore? And shoes! She had no idea she was a shoe hoarder, but remembering the sight of them all on the floor of her closet made her embarrassed. Why did one person need so many shoes? Especially since she had about five favorites that she wore ninety-five percent of time.

After reading the article, she realized that was what she wanted to do with her life. Not necessarily work at a women's shelter, but to somehow make a difference in someone's life. Going through her closet would be the first step.

It was Wednesday before she finished sorting through her clothes and started on her shoes. Why had she never done this before? She found sorting and discarding things to be therapeutic. Right as she started on her sneakers, her phone buzzed.

She didn't feel like talking with anyone, but wanted to know who it was calling. A glance at display, however, made her drop the canvas sneaker she'd been trying to decide if she should keep.

"Eric, you're calling?" She assumed he'd hit the talk button by mistake and not the text one.

"Lillian?"

Something in his tone made her stomach twist in knots, and she sat down on the floor. Had something happened to Ty? "What's going on?"

"Ty listed you as his emergency contact," Eric said, and Lillian tried to make sense of his words. They were contacting her because Ty had an emergency? Eric didn't stop, but continued, "He's in the hospital. He had what we think was a seizure, but he was very lethargic after, and disoriented."

Tight bands squeezed her insides together. She couldn't breathe, and she desperately wanted to know how he was. But when she opened her mouth, nothing came out.

"I'm in the waiting room," he said. "They just took him back. I don't have any information or other details at the moment. But I wanted you to know. I'll keep you updated."

Lillian took a deep breath. "I'm coming."

They were the only two words she could get out, but they were the only ones she needed.

Wednesday nights weren't a popular time to fly from New York to Key West, and as a result of being Isaac's PA, she had several contacts in the travel industry. Thanks to those two items, she was able to buy a nonstop, one-way ticket for a flight leaving later that night. Another call, and she had a car service in place to take her from the airport to the hospital. After tossing a few clothes and toiletries into the carryon bag she'd unpacked days earlier, she was ready.

The only thing she hadn't planned for was the three hour flight. For once, however, flying didn't bother her. Too worried to sleep and too restless to read or watch a movie, she passed almost the entire flight thinking about things she would do differently if she could go back and change them. For one, she wouldn't allow Ty to talk her into traveling home the morning after he showed up at her hotel room. She would stay in Miami even if he left and went back to Restoration. At least that way she would have been closer when he had the seizure. She could have seen with her own eyes he was fine.

Hurry. Hurry. Hurry. She implored the plane, as if it would hear and obey.

When her silent pleas didn't appear to help, she crossed her legs and bounced the top foot up and down. That lasted until she started bouncing it with more vigor and inadvertently kicked the man sitting beside her.

"Sorry," she whispered, and vowed silently to spend the rest of the flight being as still as possible.

She'd give anything to have Ty beside her now, and not just to have someone to distract her. If he was beside her, she'd know how he was doing. Eric said they thought Ty had a seizure. She searched her mind, trying to find any instance of anything resembling a seizure she might have witnessed when they'd been together, but came up with nothing.

Damn it, why weren't they there already? She bounced her foot again but stopped when the guy beside her gave her the stink eye. A glance at her watch showed there was still over an hour left until arrival. She closed her eyes and tried to settle her mind. Instead, multitude of images washed over her. Images of Ty or two of them. Their first date. Graduating from college. Getting married while he was in graduate school. The day they opened the office for business. The first apartment they bought. The trip to the Maldives he'd surprised her with.

They landed earlier than expected, and as she waited to disembark, she swore she'd walk to the hospital if the driver she'd arranged wasn't waiting for her. Who'd ever heard of a plan arriving early?

With no checked baggage to pick up, she hurried outside, following the signs to the location the hired cars waited. Again, maybe because it was a Wednesday night, there weren't many people around. Or maybe she was used to the crowds found at the New York area airports.

Regardless of the reason, she spotted her ride with no problem.

With a smile that actually felt real, she walked to where Eric stood outside of an SUV she recognized as being one of Tom's. "Did you scare off the ride I hired?" She didn't wait for him to open her door, but opened it herself, got in and threw her bag into the back seat.

"Nah," Eric said. "But Tom owns the agency and found out you had booked them to take you to the hospital from the airport." He shrugged. "I told him I'd make sure you got anywhere you needed."

"I'll be sure to thank him next time I see him. It was nice to see a familiar face when I landed."

"And you should know he won't take your money. He said there was no charge."

She could imagine how difficult it was to get Tom to change his mind about something once he'd made it up.

"In that case," she told Eric. "I'll have to get creative with my thanks."

He laughed and pulled onto a main road. Silence filled the air along with at least twenty unasked questions, but there was one she had to know the answer for. When she could no longer stand the silence, she blurted it out. "How is he?"

Eric sighed, and her chest felt tight, trying to prepare for whatever horrid thing she was getting ready to hear. "He's better. Not disoriented anymore, but it's odd," he paused longer than she thought he should. "He doesn't remember what happened."

CHAPTER 22
TY

Ty couldn't stop thinking that walking away from Lillian had been the biggest mistake of his life. That morning in the hotel, she'd said everything he'd always wanted to hear. She'd understood what he'd been trying to tell her for months. So then why did he then turn around and tell her she was the one who had been right all along, and he was the one in the wrong?

Because he was the biggest idiot who ever lived.

Ty knew it. Tom knew it. And Eric not only knew it, but told him as much when he saw Ty arrive back at headquarters.

Actually, his exact words were, "Fucking hell! What's your problem?" But Ty translated that to mean, if you're not the biggest idiot of all time, you're a close second. What's more, Ty agreed with him.

For the first few days, Ty spent his time dwelling on what he'd done wrong. It wasn't until the early hours of

Wednesday morning he realized no matter how many times he replayed the last week, he couldn't change the past. The only thing he had control over was his present, and by changing the present, he could affect the future.

He tried to get his mind to accept the thought and put it aside to deal with later in the day. Unfortunately, his mind wouldn't cooperate, and it was only an hour or so before his alarm when off that he drifted off to sleep.

Ty felt the lack of sleep with every step and every move he made later that morning. He drank three cups of coffee before climbing into the van Eric was driving. He'd hoped the caffeinated beverages would revive him enough so he didn't look like yesterday's thrown out garbage. He knew the coffee failed when Eric took one look at him and said, "Are you sure you feel up to working today? You don't look so hot."

"Wasn't able to sleep much last night," was all Ty said in response.

Eric looked over him, gave a curt nod, and said, "We're glad to have you with us, but if you need to take a break or work slower, do it and don't push yourself."

Ty nodded, and said of course, but he knew hell would need a freeze warning before he admitted to needing an extra break or less work than the others.

Everything was fine for the first few hours. No one else seemed to think anything was off with him, and though Eric glanced his way a time or two, by midmorning, he'd stopped checking. With a deep breath, Ty let his mind wonder back to what he'd been thinking about in the early morning hours, and planning the best way to confess to Lillian what an ass he'd been and beg her to take him back

He wasn't sure how much time passed when he heard Tom drive up, and Eric announced it was time to break for lunch. The temperature must have been higher than it had been. Ty didn't remember sweating as much the other days. He stood up and wiped his brow.

His arm had that pen and needles sensation like it did when he slept on it wrong. He shook it to make it stop, but it went numb.

"Ty?"

He looked to where he heard his name being called, but couldn't see who it was. They were too fuzzy. That was strange, he thought. Then his eyes closed, and he fell.

Too bright.

"Ty?"

Much too bright. He tried to tell them.

"I think he's coming around."

There were other people talking as well, but their voices were more of a buzz than actual words. Ty wasn't sure who they were talking about, but they sounded excited. Maybe he should try to see as well. He forced his eyes open against the bright light.

"Ty?"

He waited for the blurriness to fade away. And blinked.

And blinked again.

The person's face came into view at the exact same moment his head began to throb. The beating sound so intense, his body almost rocked with each pound.

"Ty?"

Ty blinked again. "Eric?" Eric was who everyone was excited about? He wished he'd kept his eyes closed. Then maybe his head wouldn't hurt so much.

Eric chuckled. "Glad to know you're really back with us this time."

Damn, he must have said that out loud.

"I heard our patient woke up," a strange feminine voice said.

It was the strangeness of the voice that made him look around. Where was he?

"Mr. Bancroft," the unknown woman said. "I'm your nurse, Wendy. You're in the hospital."

That would certainly explain why she was wearing scrubs and a white jacket.

"Why?" he thought to ask.

Wendy shared a look with Eric, who just shook his head.

"You had a seizure," Wendy said. "And then you lost consciousness. Do you remember?"

Did he? He tried to think back to what was happening before he went to sleep. He had gone to sleep, right? He didn't remember, but why else would he have woken up?

Wendy reached up and pushed a button on something above his head. That's right, she said he'd lost consciousness. But before then? He thought back to the last thing he remembered.

"It was lunch. That's what you said." Ty looked at Eric, vaguely hearing Tom's car pulling up to the worksite. The other man nodded. "I stood up."

That was all.

Wendy and Eric shared another look. Ty attempted to ignore them.

What happened after he stood up? He couldn't remember, no matter how hard he tried to get his brain to go back to the time when he was standing. "I only remember standing."

Wendy nodded and typed on the device she had in her hand. Ty couldn't help but wonder what she was typing and if his answers were good ones. What would happen if there were bad? He glanced to Eric to see if his expression gave anything away. No. He made a note to himself to never play poker with the man. His face was a blank slate.

"I'll alert the doctor on call that you're awake," Wendy said, before nodding to Eric and leaving.

"I think she likes you," Ty told Eric after the door closed behind her. He thought it telling the other man said nothing, but only shifted his feet. Ty waited, and after a few seconds ticked by, he sighed. "If you won't talk about the pretty nurse, at least tell me what happened."

Eric cleared his throat. "It started the way you said. Tom pulled up, I announced it was time for lunch, and everyone starting putting their tools away to eat. I remember you standing, but then I turned around to help Tom set up the tables. The next thing I know, everyone's shouting. When I look back, I saw Grant holding you."

Eric's voice sounded calm and even, but there was a terror lurking behind his eyes that told TY he wasn't either of the two. Whatever had happened, or whatever Ty had done, had left a mark on him.

"Grant said after you stood up, you shook your hand like you were trying to get something off. Then, suddenly, your eyes rolled back in your head and you fell. Luckily, he was working close to you and had enough presence of mind and quick enough reflexes that he caught you before you landed and cracked your head on something. I ran over to help him. By the time I got there, you were seizing."

Jesus. Why couldn't Ty remember any of this? "I don't know what happened," he said, and almost felt as if he should apologize. Maybe if he said he was sorry, it would ease the shell-shocked look Eric still carried. "I don't remember anything like this happening before."

Don't you, though? Something whispered in the back of his mind.

Eric nodded. "I keep the medical forms of all the volunteers in the van for that exact reason. I kept thinking I must have missed something on your form, but I pulled it, and it said no known medical conditions."

Ty wondered if he should mention the other time he woke up and discovered there were parts of the recent past he couldn't recall? But no, he didn't want to burden Eric with that information. He wouldn't know what to do with it, anyway. It'd better for him to wait and discuss it with the doctor when he stopped by.

And maybe, just maybe, he'd finally get some closure about that night three years ago.

"There's something I need to tell you," Eric said.

Ty couldn't understand the guilt in his voice or the way Eric found it difficult to meet his gaze. "Okay."

"Lillian was listed on your medical form as your emergency contact."

It took a few seconds for it to sink in that there was a reason Eric felt the need to remind him of that fact. Ty blamed the alleged seizure for making his brain work slower than normal, but when he finally realized what Eric was really saying, he cursed. "And you called her, didn't you?"

"At the time, we didn't know what we were dealing with," Eric said. "We thought it might be a seizure, but you were so lethargic and disoriented... I was worried. You listed her as the person to call if there was an emergency. This qualified."

Ty's head still pounded, and it hurt to think, but there was something Eric had just said that he knew he needed to question. "I was lethargic and disoriented?" He asked when it hit him. "I wasn't unconscious the entire time?"

"No," Eric said. "You were conscious once before the ambulance showed up. You don't remember any of it?"

"Not a bit," he confirmed. "Did I say or do anything?"

"You didn't walk around or anything. You talked, or at least you tried to. No one could understand what you were saying."

Ty couldn't help but wonder if this solved the mystery of what happened three years ago. Was it possible he'd had a similar episode, and no one told him? That didn't seem likely. Unless Jessica was the only one in the apartment with him at the time. Which meant...

Holy fuck! Had she undressed both of them and somehow got them into bed? Or had he moved of his own accord? And if it had been a seizure, why hadn't he had one in three years? He was suddenly eager for the doctor to come in.

"About Lillian..." Eric said.

"What about her?"

"She's on her way here, and should arrive in about four hours."

CHAPTER 23
LILLIAN

Lillian had rarely felt as nervous as she did when Eric pulled into the parking lot of the hospital. The last time she'd seen TY, he left little doubt about his thoughts on the two of them getting or staying together. But, she argued with herself, just because he didn't want to be with her didn't mean they weren't still friends, right? Although friends seemed too clinical of a word to describe what they were. No matter. Even if they weren't together romantically, they were still allowed to care what happened to the other.

"Lillian?" Eric asked, raising an eyebrow in her direction.

She realized she hadn't unbuckled her seat belt yet. "I hope he's not upset I came. I keep telling myself, I was the person he put down as his emergency contact. But I know he never in a million years thought it'd be needed."

Eric looked at her with an intensity that left her feeling self-conscious. She forced herself to remain still under his gaze.

"I wasn't sure if I should tell you or not." He looked away, running a hand through his hair. With a sigh, he turned back to her. "But I think you should know. I think you have a right to know. The thing is, after his seizure, he gained consciousness before they brought him to the hospital. He wasn't mobile, but he spoke. Most of it, we couldn't make out. But there were a few words we could, and one of them was your name."

"My name?"

"Yes," Eric confirmed. "But you have to know, he doesn't remember anything during the time just before the seizure until he woke up in the hospital."

"So you're telling me he won't remember saying my name, is that it?"

"Partially," he said. "But more than that... Look, I'm no relationship expert. I've had one long-term relationship, and I engage in sexual activities a good portion of people find unacceptable, but I know when two people belong together. I don't know why you and TY divorced, and I don't want to know, The thing is, I can't help but think whatever tore you apart, surely can't outweigh the emotion I see between you two."

"What are you saying?"

"I see the way the two of you look at each other, particularly when you think no one's watching. I have to admit,

I'm a little jealous." The corner of his mouth lifted in a half smile. "It'd be nice to have someone look at me that way."

She wanted to tell him she was certain someone would one day, but held back because it sounded trite in her head. "You can't build a life off of a look."

"No," he agreed. "But what you can do is build a bridge and meet each other in the middle of it."

She repeated his words to herself while walking down the hallway toward Ty's room. Eric had given her the number and then told her he'd be in the waiting room. Ty's door was cracked open a little, and she hesitated for a second to listen and ensure no one else was inside other than him. She let half a minute go by before she knocked.

"Come in," Ty said from inside.

She took a deep breath and pushed the door open. "Hey, you."

"Lillian." He was sitting up in the bed, and, aside from looking paler than normal, he appeared the same as he did the last time she saw him. "Eric told me you were coming. I'm fine. You didn't have to, you know, you could have just called."

"I don't care. A phone call isn't the same. I had to see you with my own eyes."

"I know," he said, and a smile teased his lips. "And I'm glad you did."

She wasn't expecting him to say that and didn't know how to reply, so she changed the subject. "You look good. When are they going to let you go?"

He sighed. "I was hoping tonight, but they're still waiting on tests results and they aren't coming until tomorrow. Assuming they don't show anything unexpected, I'll be released then."

"Are you going back to work with Restoration?"

He shook his head. "No. The doctor advised me not to. I'd like to, though. Unfortunately, Eric overheard what the doctor said, and he told me I'm not allowed onsite."

"Will you go home to New York?"

He gave her an odd look she couldn't read. "I haven't decided yet. Where are you staying tonight?"

She hadn't made hotel reservations because she'd been unsure about how he'd be when she landed. With a nod toward the one chair in the room, she said, "That chair looks comfy."

"You can't sleep in a chair all night."

"This thing with you telling me what I am and am not going to do is tiresome and needs to stop. I'm staying in the chair."

He must have heard the determination in her voice because he didn't attempt to change her mind again. "Maybe I'll spend a few days in Florida before heading back home. It's been a frightfully long time since I've had a vacation."

"That would be good for you." Lillian skirted around the foot of the bed to the chair and sat down. "What are the doctors saying?"

"That it's something genetic, probably exacerbated by stress and lack of sleep. If I can keep my stress down and take proper care of myself, there's the potential I might be able to ward off another one."

"That doesn't sound too bad," she said. Relatively speaking, it could be a lot worse. "Did they say anything about your memory?" Which wasn't the question she wanted to ask at all, but she couldn't get her mouth to wrap around the words of the one she did.

"He said I might get back, and I might not." Ty snorted. "Said the brain was a mysterious organ, and man had yet to unlock all of its secrets."

She wrinkled her forehead. "That's a strange thing for a doctor to say, don't you think?"

"It was rather refreshing, I thought. For him not to pretend he had all the answers and knew everything."

Lillian supposed that made sense. She needed to ask her question. To find out if it was a seizure he had the night of the party. But as much as she wanted to know, she likewise didn't want to know. If what she saw when she opened the bedroom door that night had resulted from a medical condition, she was the worst sort of scum there was. You didn't divorce someone over a medical condition they had zero control over.

"I mentioned to him I had another similar episode a few years back," Ty said, lifting the burden of having to ask from her. Tears threatened to fall because she knew how the doctor would respond. "He told me it was possible, that in fact, it was more than likely the same thing, but we would never know with any certainty."

She didn't need the doctor's certainty. She knew that's what had caused everything. Which made her the world's nastiest bitch.

"Don't do it, Lillian."

Her head jerked up.

"Don't think what you're thinking. I won't allow it," he said in his no nonsense voice. "I don't care what you say about it getting tiresome."

"How do you know what I'm thinking?"

"You're feeling guilty about the divorce and believing I cheated on you." His stare was unnerving in that delightful way Dom's had at staring at a submissive. "There was no reason for you to think it was anything other than what you saw."

A tear rolled down her cheek. "No reason except I knew you would never cheat."

"I don't blame you," he said. "I don't hold you in any way responsible for anything that happened."

"You're too nice, you know?" She wiped her eyes. "Someone's going to take advantage of you one day."

"You can take advantage of me any time you want."

"I thought you wanted me to fall in love with Eric because you were afraid if you and I got back together we'd tarnish each other or some such ridiculousness."

"I said a damn lot of ridiculous things in my life, but that one was over the top."

A beacon of hope began to burn in her heart. "You don't want me to fall in love with Eric?"

"Hell, no," he said. "Besides, I'm pretty sure he's smitten with my nurse."

She couldn't remember him ever using the word smitten before, and that he did, made her laugh. "What about us tarnishing each other?"

"Oh," he said. "I'm pretty sure we'll tarnish each other. In fact, I plan to tarnish you every chance I get."

"Why would you do that?"

Though his voice was deadpan when he answered, his eyes danced in mischief. "Because then I get to clean you up. And I love taking a shower with you."

CHAPTER 24
TY

After being released from the hospital, Ty suggested they spend a few days at the hotel Lillian had left days prior. They both laughed when they were given the same suite as before.

He'd brought up delaying the trip back to New York because he thought it was important to be alone together before getting bombarded by the many questions their friends and colleagues would assuredly have. Besides, he told her; he wasn't ready to go back to work yet.

"Why not?" Lillian asked him as they sat drinking coffee on the balcony overlooking the ocean.

It was a good question, but not one he had a definitive answer for. He had a few ideas that might explain his hesitancy.

"It doesn't have anything to do with me, does it?" She asked, and he realized he'd never replied to her question.

"No." He reached over and put his hand on top of hers. "It has nothing to do with you. It's all me." She nodded, but he got the impression she did so out of habit as opposed to believing him. "I mean it. There's something I've been thinking about, especially since working with Restoration. Sitting here made me realize I'd like to know your thoughts as well."

She looked wary, but asked, "Thoughts on what?"

He took a deep breath because it hit him he didn't know how she would react. "I've been tossing around selling my portion of the business to Isaac and, or Lance."

Her jaw dropped. "Why?"

Why? It was a question he'd been asking himself, and now that Lillian had the same, he hoped to find some answers.

"It probably makes me an ass, like I don't appreciate all I've been given," he said. "But that's not why. The truth is, I want more."

Lillian's forehead wrinkled. "More what?"

"I want my life to be about more than how much money I can make. I have plenty." He moved his hand from her and shifted his chair so he could lean closer to her. "It keeps me up at night sometimes. When my life is over, what will I leave behind other than a lot of money?"

She stared at him with an odd look on her face. He wasn't sure if it was what he said or if she'd somehow misheard him.

When he couldn't stop himself, he asked, "What?"

"Who are you?"

He smiled at her question. "I'm still me. Why are you looking at me like that?"

"I've never seen this side of you before, and it's shocking because I thought I knew you inside and out."

At least she wasn't looking at him like he had two heads anymore. "It didn't hit me until I was in London. Even then, I didn't know what my problem was. I thought it was the combination of the divorce and the move. The closest I can come to describing what it felt like would be wearing clothes that didn't fit quite right or having your shoes on the wrong feet. I knew something wasn't right, and even though I was uncomfortable, I could put up with it. But working with Restoration opened my eyes to what my problem is. I want to do something other than write a check for an organization. I want to get my hands dirty."

"That might be the hottest thing I've ever heard come out of your mouth," she said.

Ty chuckled. "I find that very hard to believe."

"Did you know I haven't had a job since resigning from the office?"

"No," he said. In fact, he couldn't imagine Lillian not working. She was type person who had to always be busy. "What have you been doing?" He asked, not to imply she was lounging around all day, though working for Isaac as long as she had, she certainly deserved to do just that. No, he asked because couldn't fathom how she spent her time.

"For the first few days, all I did was sleep." She laughed, but he didn't find it funny at all.

"Next time I see Isaac, I'm going to kick his ass for working you into exhaustion," he said.

"No, you won't." She leveled her gaze at him. "I didn't do anything I didn't want to."

He waved his hand in dismissal, not wanting to discuss his business partner. "I'll give him a pass this time. What did you do when you woke up?"

"I tried to figure out what it was I wanted to do with my life."

"And did you?"

"No," she said. "But when I got home after leaving Maimi, I cleaned out my closet. It was a mess because have done nothing to it since I moved in other than to add more stuff to it. I had so much stuff. It was embarrassing when I saw everything I had in there and knowing how little of it I wore. I had to do something. As it turns out, there's a women's shelter, close to your office, and they not only give them a place to live, but they also teach life skills and help them find jobs. Apparently, they're always needing clothes for when the women go on job interviews. I had finished my clothes and had those packed and ready to go. In fact, I was making a pretty good dent getting my shoes together to go, when I got the call from Eric about you."

"Coming here kept you from finishing your donation," he said. "I'm sorry."

"Don't apologize. It's not like you had a seizure on purpose, and everything will still be in the spot I left it when I get back home. But the point of that wasn't to tell you about my closet. It was because it was while I was packing the boxes of clothes, I kept thinking about how awesome it would be to help someone in a more tangible way. Sort of like you said to do more than to only be the person who gives the clothes."

"Who are you?" he asked when she finished.

She threw her seat cushion at him.

CHAPTER 25
LILLIAN

Ty looked over at her with an I can't believe you just did that look on his face. "Oh, Lilli," he said in his serious as hell Dom voice that electrified her all over. "Did you just throw something at me?"

They hadn't talked yet about rekindling the BDSM portion of their relationship, and his use of her submissive name caught her off guard as much as it turned her on. She realized she was gaping at him when the corner of his mouth quirked up.

"You can tell me no," he said, but she inferred he wasn't talking about the question he'd just asked.

She could tell him no if she wasn't ready to engage in that dynamic with him yet, or if she needed more time to ensure she could trust him. If she told him no, he would respect her answer and wouldn't nag her to change her mind.

On the other hand...

If she said yes, they could begin again, but stronger and sturdier than before. Was it a risk? Of course it was, but a life without risk was boring. One thing Lillian could say with certainty was that life with Ty would never be boring.

He watched her with careful eyes, as if uncertain about her response. Though she believed deep down, he knew.

She gave an exaggerated yawn. "Yes. What are you going to do about it?" She bit the inside of her cheek to stop the laugh threatening to burst out of her at his growl.

He stood and walked to the foot of her lounger. "Come here."

Her heart raced while her body hurried to obey, excited about where he was going to take this. When she stood before him, she didn't hesitate before going to her knees. Once in position, it seemed as if everything in her world fell into place. She closed her eyes and took a deep breath. On her exhale, she let go of the past, and with that simple action, a weight she'd unknowingly carried for the last few years lifted and was gone.

"I'm not sure I've ever seen you smile so big," Ty said above her.

She kept her eyes closed. Silly, she knew, but she feared the feeling would disappear if she opened them. "I've never felt so.... light.... and free."

He dug his fingers into her hair and started a soothing massage. She nearly moaned in pleasure. Head massages were her favorite, and Ty always gave the best ones. Somewhere along the way, she'd forgotten how good it felt.

He chuckled. "Still like that, do you?"

"Mmm," was all she could get out.

"I remember other things you enjoyed as well."

She kept silent because she enjoyed damn near everything they did together.

"Stand and undress from the waist down," he said, as if asking for a glass of water.

Her eyes flew open, and she looked up at him, but he didn't repeat himself. He never did. He crossed his arms and looked at her with a raised eyebrow.

She took her time standing, and then, keeping her eyes on his the entire time, slipped off her shorts and underwear, letting them land wherever they fell.

"Very nice, Lilli," he said, his eyes growing dark as he took the sight of her in. "Go lean across the railing."

They were on the top floor and even though she knew no one could see them because of the way the various floors and buildings and floors were arranged, it still felt hedonistic. Did she really feel that free?

"Are you sure you're up to this?" she asked. "They only released you from the hospital this morning."

He unzipped his shorts and drew them down over his hip. Unlike her, he didn't have any underwear on. "Does it appear as if I'm up for it?"

She eyed his erection. "All your parts appear to be fully operational."

"I assure you they are," he said with a hint of a smile. "So while I appreciate the concern, please note for future reference that I'm very aware of my limits."

If she thought hard enough about it, she'd be able to come up with more things to argue about, but the truth of the matter was, after seeing how hard he was, arguing was the last thing on her mind.

"In that case," she said, walking past him to the railing. "Come here and give it to me."

No sooner had she got into position, than Ty was behind her. He rotated his hips to let her feel the length of him.

"Feel how hard you make me?" His hands slipped between her legs and he groaned at what he found. "Because I feel how wet you are for me."

It was true, she'd never again deny how responsive she was to Ty. She pushed her hips back, not wanting foreplay or verbal spats or anything other than him inside her. The fact he didn't smack her ass or tell her to wait until he was ready, showed how much he needed her as well.

He pushed inside her with a thrust that sent her upper body slamming into the stone railing. Good thing it was stone, he might have shattered it had it been wood. There was nothing sweet or gentle like before. He didn't relent or slow down, pounding into her harder and harder, claiming every inch of her. Just when she thought he couldn't get any deeper, he'd adjust his angle or shift her hips a bit, and she'd be proven wrong.

"Look at that, down there," he said, his breathing only slightly ragged.

She opened her eyes, look down, and gasped.

Ty chuckled. "I'll admit, I made sure no one could see us from their room, but I forgot the people on the ground could see us if they looked up."

She knew he'd done no such thing. Ty wasn't one to forget things like that. He'd wanted to wait until this exact moment to bring it up.

"As long as you're quiet and don't scream or anything, we should be fine," he whispered.

Of course, she had no problem being silent before he mentioned the potential of being seen by people on the ground. Now, with his every thrust, every scrape of the rough stone on her exposed skin, and every grunt he gave as he fucked her harder and faster had her gritting her teeth against the whimpers of pleasure that would surely turn to screams if she allowed even the tiniest of peeps out.

Just when she thought she had herself under control, Ty started talking in a low grumble.

"Fuck, you're so tight around my dick."

"Spread your legs wider, Lilli. I think I can go a little deeper.... oh fuck, yeah, just like that."

Her body trembled with her approaching climax. She wasn't going to be able to hold it back. And it was going to be loud. "Ty," she panted. "I can't be quiet... I can't..."

She wasn't sure he heard her until he suddenly pulled out, lifted her into his arms and carried her through the door they'd thankfully left open, leading to the bedroom. He lifted her to where only her upper body was on the bed and hooked her legs over his shoulder. Holy fuck, he was going to hit everything in that position.

"Let me hear you scream," he said before fucking his cock into her so hard and deep, she saw stars. Orgasm hit her so hard and fast, she couldn't tell if she screamed or not. Ty pumped his hips one more time and held still deep inside for his own release.

"Holy shit," he said, pulling them further up the bed and then collapsing beside her. "I think you killed me."

"Me?" she asked. "You almost killed me and got me arrested for indecent exposure."

"I don't think anyone would have been able to see you even if you'd screamed."

"How's that?" Because from where she'd been standing, all they would have had to do was to look up.

"I don't think they would have seen anything that way."

"Why?"

"Because I checked out the angle when we were outside walking on the beach. The architecture is incredible."

It shouldn't surprise her he'd thought to check something like that, but it always did. Sitting up, she reached for the bottle of water on the nightstand, causing her thighs to protest. "Ow," she said. "I didn't realize sex involved otherwise unused muscles."

"Are you sore?"

"Only a little, and nothing I can't handle." She didn't want to give him the impression she couldn't handle a second round.

He placed a hand on her thigh. "Are you sure?"

"Before the last week, I hadn't had sex in three years," she said. "Do you really think I'm going to let a few sore muscles stop me now?"

"You really haven't been with anyone since the divorce?" He reached across her to get the water bottle she wanted.

"No one." She took a big swallow of the water. "At first it was because I worked so much, or at least that's what I told myself. The truth was, I didn't want anyone other than you."

He swept a piece of hair out of her face. "I know how you feel."

She raised an eyebrow at him. "How's that?"

"How many women do you think I've been with since the divorce?"

"I don't know." She wrinkled her forehead. "Between three and five?"

"Try zero."

CHAPTER 26
TY

Ty supposed her shock shouldn't surprise him. Everyone else he'd talked with assumed he'd become a man-whore after Lillian left him, though he never could understand why they would think such a thing.

"I won't say I never dated, because I did. Hell, you remember Janice went with me." At her nod, he continued. "And you know how my sister is, always trying to set people up. God, sometimes that woman drove me up the wall. So, yeah, I went out a few times, but nothing else."

She still had the gobsmacked look on her face. "But you were always such a sexual person."

"As were you," he pointed out. "Looks as though we were both only sexual with each other."

She smiled at that, he was pleased to note. "That makes sense."

He watched her and couldn't help but wonder if she truly understood. "What you and I have is beyond anything physical." Using only one finger, he traced her lips, then drew his finger downward, brushing her collarbone, before dragging his fingertip to the sensitive spot in the crook of elbow.

She shivered delightfully.

"Do you think any other woman would respond to my touch that way?"

"Eventually."

"You really think so?" He swirled his finger around one of her nipples and enjoyed the moan she gave in response. It turned him on so much, he lowered his head and sucked it into his mouth. Hearing her sharp intake of breath, he bit it gently. That time she yelped. "Because I don't think anyone else would even come close."

She remained silent, but there were still doubts in her eyes.

"Come here," he said, pulling her into his lap. His hands skimmed her curves. "No one else has a body made for me alone." He took her hand and placed it on his length, already hard again. "No one else does this to me."

She scooted down, looking at him with questions in her eyes. She wanted to take him in her mouth and was looking for permission. As much as he loved watching her lips around his dick as he pushed into her mouth, it wouldn't happen right now.

"Later," he told her. "I won't last two seconds if you so much as breathe on me." It wasn't an exaggeration. "Come here and sit on my cock."

She took her time situating herself so she straddled him. Then, ever so slowly, she eased her way onto his cock. He loved this position. No matter if she rode him or if he held her hips still and steady as he fucked her.

This time, however, once she'd taken him all the way inside, he stopped her. He wanted to ensure she didn't move, but felt every inch he had inside her. "Do you feel me inside you? Feel the way I fill you up? I can't do this with another woman. Being inside you is more than a physical act. It's so much more. I only want this connection with you, and if that's not possible for whatever reason, I'm fine not having it all. I love you, and only you." He removed his hands. "Now ride me. Do it slow so you take in every sensation."

She had tears running down her cheeks, but she obeyed him, and even though he'd like nothing more than to drive himself into her over and over, he let her lead. He wanted her to search and discover her own truth in their union.

He knew she'd found it when she moved, demanding more from herself and demanding more from him. He willingly gave her everything he had, holding on to her, and watching as she drove them.

She was fierce and forceful, striving for her pleasure and using his body to find it. He'd never experienced anything hotter, and as soon as her climax hit, he was right behind her.

For several minutes they didn't move. If it were possible for them to stay the way they were right this minute, wrapped up in each other, no outside worries or troubles, he'd do it. But he knew all too well the impossibility of that.

Which left them with only one other option.

"Lillian?" he asked.

"Mmm," she muttered against his chest.

"Marry me."

Her eyes flew open. "Are you serious?"

"Never been more serious in my life," he said. "In fact, I don't want to wait. Let's do it here. Before we go back home."

"You've lost your mind."

"I know. Will you have me anyway?"

She laughed. "Yes."

EPILOGUE
LILLIAN

Eight Months Later

Lillian looked around the table at the people who meant the most to her. Lance and Celeste. Isaac and Maggie. And, of course, Ty. They were having dinner at Windows, a new restaurant in Manhattan. Though the building the restaurant occupied the top floor of wasn't the tallest in the city, when you looked out of the floor to ceiling windows of the private dining room on the seventy-eighth floor, you didn't care.

Conversation at the table was animated. Though that was expected whenever the six friends got together, it was even more so tonight. No doubt, because of the wedding tomorrow.

Lance and Celeste were glowing, Lillian thought. She'd first met the young woman who'd captured Lance's attention so quickly during her audition for his family's scholarship at his Grandmother Barbara's house. If you'd told her then the calm and quiet young woman would have ended up his wife, she'd have laughed her ass off.

Lillian also remembered having a conversation with Lance not long after that first meeting in which he mentioned his concern with their seventeen year age difference. She was glad to see that no longer bothered him. Twenty-seven-year-old Celeste had confided in Lillian since then that she'd always had a thing for older men. After turning twenty, she'd said, she dated no one less than ten years older, claiming guys her own age were idiots.

However, Lance and Celeste weren't the most unexpected couple in the world. No, that honor definitely belonged to the other couple at the table. Isaac Gregory was as much as a Type A, perfectionist as one could get. Everyone had long given up on him ever settling down because, frankly, no one thought anyone would ever meet his insanely high ideals. Then Maggie walked in, or more accurately, she walked into him. She was yin to his yang, the chaos to his control. Lillian wasn't sure how they did it, but it somehow worked.

In fact, Lillian couldn't say with certainty because Maggie had been keeping her left hand in her lap for most of the night, but she thought she'd seen a quick flash of sparkle on one of the few times she brought her hand to the table.

"I'm glad we all agreed to do this instead of the traditional bachelor and bachelorette parties," Lance said as they finished up dinner. "Dinner with your best friends is better than getting shit-faced and doing who knows what."

"Speak for yourself," Celeste said. "I wouldn't have minded a few half-naked men dancing around."

"I can still make that happen," Maggie quipped.

"No you can't," Lance and Isaac said at the same time.

Ty laughed. "I think she should do it. It'd be fun to watch."

"You think it'd be fun to watch a bunch of half-naked men dance?" Lillian asked him.

"Hell, no. It'd be fun to watch Lance and Isaac," he said, and everyone except Lance and Isaac laughed.

"And why weren't we able to torment you with the idea of being entertained by male strippers?" Lance asked, then slapped his head as if remembering. "Oh, that's right, because we weren't even invited to your wedding."

"It was eight months ago, Lance, and we didn't invite anyone," Lillian said. "Seriously, let it go."

Ty shrugged at his old friend. "I can't help that I'm smarter than you."

"It may have been smart, but it was a shit move," Lance said. "We're your best friends, we wanted to celebrate with you."

Lance was only teasing, of course. All four of them had been thrilled when she and Ty made it back to New York and announced their newly remarried status.

"I think it's romantic," Celeste said from his side with a sigh. "The two of you deciding you have to get married at once. That you can't wait another second."

"Wish I'd known that before we sent out five hundred invitations for tomorrow," Lance teased his soon-to-be wife, who punched his upper arm in response.

"It sounds more romantic than it was," Lillian said. "We found out that you have to wait three days to marry after obtaining a license in Florida."

TY slipped his arm across her shoulders. "I told her that was fine, we'd just go to Georgia. I'd always wanted to see Savannah, anyway."

"Except he wanted to leave that night." Lillian rolled her eyes. "Keep in mind, he had been in the hospital just that morning, and it was a seven hour drive to Savannah. I didn't think it'd be a good idea for him to drive, and I'd slept in a chair the night before, and didn't trust myself to drive that long being sleep deprived. That's not even taking into account Ty would be in charge of navigating if I drove, and we know that will never happen again."

"Why is that?" Maggie asked, and Isaac leaned over to whisper to her. "That sounds like something I'd do," she said with a giggle when he'd finished.

"Duly noted," Isaac said. "No navigating for you."

"You didn't think about flying?" Celeste asked.

"Lillian doesn't like to fly," Ty explained. "Good thing you came back to the States to get married."

"You know, I'd have been there if you got married in London," Lillian said. "I'd be doped up, but I'd have been there."

"I know you would have," Celeste said. "By the way, I keep meaning to ask, how's the nonprofit coming?"

Lance and Isaac had refused to buy Ty completely out. In the end, Ty agreed to keep twenty-five percent of his share of the company, and to continue his spot on the Board of Directors. Lillian agreed it was the best deal for all concerned. Ty could keep his hands in the business and still move on with starting a non-profit with her.

"It's going well," Lillian told her. "Taking more time to get it up and running, but because of the scope, we want to ensure nothing's missed. Besides, Isaac's on the Oversight Committee, and you know he's picky as shit."

"I heard that," Isaac said.

"I would hope so, since you're sitting right there," Lillian said.

In a surprising turn of fate, Tom would serve on the same committee. Shortly after they arrived back to New York, Lillian searched for information on the kind and unassuming gentleman who seemed to own quite a bit of property. He turned out to be Thomas Goodell, a business guru who had made a fortune in real estate, but now enjoyed giving that fortune away.

"What else would I do with it?" he'd asked Lillian. "I never married or had any kids, and I sure as hell don't want the government to get it when I die."

It only seemed right to ask him to serve on a board of their nonprofit. The Bancroft Group, as they named it, would work to bring businesses needing interns and apprentices together with people from under represented communities. They also had a plan to work with high schools to ensure graduating students had the resources to create a career plan and a definitive way to start on that plan.

The unmistakable ping of a glass being tapped with a piece of silverware drew her attention to Lance.

"Excuse me," he said, standing and placing the glass and fork down.

There hadn't been that much chatter in the room, or at least that had been Lillian's thinking before the absolute silence that fell upon the room when Lance stood up.

"Wow," he said. "I'll have to remember how well that works to shut you guys up."

Isaac flipped him the bird.

Lance laughed. "But seriously, you guys. Thank you for all you've done. Tomorrow wouldn't have been possible without you. And for your information, and in case anyone was ever to ask, Celeste and I do not recommend planning a wedding from a different country."

Celeste nodded at his side. "A to the men."

"I've been blessed with a wonderful family, friends that are closer than family, and above all, the love of a woman who is way out of my league, but said yes to me, anyway." He turned to the blushing woman by his side. "Celeste, I love you. You are the song I want to spend the rest of my life singing."

Lance bent down to kiss her.

Lillian turned to whisper to Ty that she had no idea Lance could be so romantic, but a sparkle of reflected light caught her attention. It was Maggie, wiping her eyes with both hands. The left one sporting a brilliant diamond that wasn't there when the two of them had lunch last week.

"Looks like Isaac was able to convince Maggie to come around to his way of thinking," Lillian whispered to Ty.

Maggie, hard as it was to believe, was a widow, and had been hesitant to walk down that path again. Apparently, she'd worked through whatever had been holding her back.

"Looks like," Ty agreed. "It's good to see everyone happy and settling down."

Lillian took his hand and thought back over the last eight months. Everything was right in her life again. "Do you think they're as happy as you and me?"

"Doubtful," he murmured, closing in to kiss her. "No one could ever be that happy."

As his lips brushed hers, she knew he told the truth.

FOK
SEE HOW IT ALL STARTED

FOK: (noun) /fok/: Abbreviation for Fill-or-Kill, a term used in securities trading. To fulfill an order completely and immediately, or to not do it at all.

For Lance Braxton, it's more than a trading term, it's his motto. Do it. Do it now and do it completely or don't do it at all. Some might see it as reckless or foolhardy, but Lance doesn't care. It's worked for him so far. Why change a good thing?

As a favor for his sick grandmother, Lance sits in on auditions for the Juilliard scholarship named after his late mother. He expects to be bored out of his mind. He expects it to be a waste of a Saturday he could spend working. What he does not expect is Celeste Walsh.

She has the body of a super model, the looks of a storybook princess, and plays the violin with the passion of a zealous lover. The moment he sees her, he has to have her. Wants to control her. Needs to master her.

Celeste Walsh is running out of options. She's been accepted into Juilliard to play the violin, but if she can't get a scholarship, she'll have to turn them down. And if she turns Juilliard down, she'll have no choice but to give up the violin and work as a waitress at her family's restaurant in Nowhereville, Virginia.

She's not sure accepting the scholarship is the smartest thing to do. There's something about the way Lance looks at her that suggests he has more than arias and scherzos in mind. However, when she inadvertently witnesses an intimate moment between him and a date, she realizes being under his control holds more appeal than she thought.

Lance warns her he's an all or nothing guy and if she steps into his bedroom, he's not holding back. It's not until her foot crosses the threshold that she understands just how serious he is. But even if she comes to trust him with her pleasure, does she dare trust him with her heart?

Chapter One

In her mind, Celeste Walsh was a badass. She never backed down, never averted her gaze first, and never took shit from anyone.

In reality, however, though she refused to be a doormat, she had yet to blossom into full-blown badassery. The closest she'd been able to get was to perfect the art of remaining utterly calm in the face of anything. Her roommate, Reagan, told her it was her superpower. Celeste had snorted and said if that was true, she wanted to exchange it for something useful, like mind reading or invisibility.

Although, she had to admit that today this odd superpower could come in handy. She was auditioning for a scholarship, but that wasn't anything new. In fact, this was her eleventh scholarship audition. What made this audition different was that it would be the last. Last audition. Her last hope.

If she didn't score this scholarship, she wouldn't be attending Juilliard in the fall. Which would also mean no longer being able to stay in New York. She'd be on a bus headed back home to Middle-of-Nowhere Virginia. Upon arrival, her parents would put her to work, either washing dishes or bussing tables at the family's farm to table restaurant.

She shivered, determined to get this one.

"Hey, Celeste," one of her fellow applicants, Erin, said.

Celeste smiled and greeted the young woman in a similar financial situation as her own. They'd auditioned at many of the same scholarships and had received rejections from the same ones. There were a few they hadn't heard from yet.

"Did you hear?" Erin asked, her eyes dancing the way they did when she wanted to share the latest juicy gossip.

"Probably not." Celeste rarely listened to gossip or watched the news. Her life revolved around the violin. Violin. School. Violin. She possessed little time for anything else in her life. And she didn't apologize or make excuses for it. Especially with the new piece she planned for today's audition.

"Barbara Murphy is in the hospital," Erin said.

"Really?" Celeste asked. That wasn't gossip. Barbara Murphy headed and funded the scholarship they were auditioning for today, in memory of her daughter. Melinda Murphy had been a pianist and had also attended Juilliard years ago when she was younger. She'd died young, but Celeste wasn't sure if she'd ever heard how. "Who's running the audition?"

"No one I've talked with knows."

They both turned to look at the auditorium doors. The first group to audition, vocalists, had entered only five minutes ago. It wasn't long before the doors opened and three guys walked out.

"Fucking asshole," the tallest one said and the other two nodded and murmured in agreement.

"Who's running the audition with Mrs. Murphy in the hospital?" Someone nearby asked.

"Her grandson," the tall guy answered. "Some Wall Street hotshot who doesn't know shit about the arts."

The trio of vocalists left amid a growing rumble of discontent. A discontent that, unfortunately, remained in their wake. However, Celeste felt no need to continue talking about the grandson she couldn't do anything about. She retreated to her corner of the room and tried to tune out the noise around her like she always did, by picturing herself playing the violin.

Knowing this was her last audition and one of the largest scholarships offered, she'd changed her audition piece. The composer wasn't as well know as the ones her competition would play, nor was the piece itself known by very many outside the music world. If this grandson was as clueless as the vocalist had alluded to, should she play something more well known?

She forced herself to breathe deep and calm. As she did, the music she needed to play made itself known. When a harried assistant called for her group, Celeste rose from her seat, lost in the calm, ready to play, and with no worries about a grandson who may or may not know the difference between a violin and a cello.

Lance Braxton cut the violinist off after nine seconds of playing. "That's enough. Next!"

Beside him, his grandmother's personal assistant, Richard, sighed and signaled for a ten minute break. Lance raised an eyebrow at him, and Richard took a deep breath before turning to address the man at his side. "Mr. Braxton, you can't cut them off like that. You must allow them to finish playing."

Lance placed his pen on the table, so it lined up exactly parallel to the pad it was next to. Only when he was certain it rested precisely where he wanted, did he turn to the man his grandmother said she couldn't operate without. "Richard," he said slowly, as if gathering his thoughts. Which he wasn't. "Perhaps you have nothing better to do today than to sit here and listen to Tchaikovsky over and over, but some of us have actual work to do."

Richard opened his mouth as if he would interrupt, but Lance shot him a look that made him change his mind. "You have worked for my grandmother for three years; however, I have been her grandson for much longer. Do you understand?"

Richard was smart enough to only nod.

"Though I do not typically sit here and listen, I know the characteristics my grandmother requires for the recipient of the scholarship bearing my mother's name. Therefore, if I determine an applicant has none of these characteristics, I'm doing us all a favor by not wasting time and letting that person go."

Lance estimated Richard cost him valuable time by putting him in a position to explain himself. He rarely explained himself. Even rarer did he do so to anyone's personal assistant. The fact he'd just done so, and that there were people who could hear the conversation, irritated him. He needed to move this thing along. He had real work to do. Though he couldn't deny his grandmother's request when she asked him to take her place today. His Grandmother Murphy was the one person he couldn't tell no.

Beside him, Richard swallowed and sweat beaded on his forehead. "Yes, Mr. Braxton. I understand."

Lance nodded. "You're excused. I'll finish up here."

The other man scrambled to pick up his notebook and pens. Lance waited with a patience he didn't feel until the door closed behind the assistant his grandmother insisted was a lifesaver. He didn't see how, but Richard wasn't his problem. At least on most days. Today, he'd been a major pain in the ass.

"Let's go, people," he said to no one in particular, knowing someone would hear and usher out the next applicant. He shuffled the papers in front of him. How many more did he have to sit through?

The click of heels on the stage alerted him the next applicant was in place. He pulled the information sheet he had on whoever it was. "Name?" He asked without looking up.

"Celeste Walsh."

Her voice was delicate and feminine. Yet something in her tone spoke of a quietly held strength. It intrigued him and he looked up. She was stunning for lack of a better word. At some point her dark hair had been pulled up, now, however, more than a few strands had fallen free, giving her a wild and untamed appearance.

An appearance that should have been at odds with her elegant yet subtle black floor length dress, but somehow wasn't. In fact, her entire ensemble could be described as a hot mess. Instead she was one of the hottest women he'd seen in a long time.

She stood waiting, the very epitome of calm, violin in hand as if she had all the time in the world. Not at all as if he held her future in his hands, which he did based upon the paper in front of him.

He wanted to crush the paper. Because in doing so he would have no ties to the glorious creature before him. Which meant he could do any damn thing she would allow him to do to her. And he'd make sure she wanted the same things he did.

But he couldn't do that, so he cleared his throat and said, "Whenever you're ready, Ms. Walsh."

She gave him a curt nod, closed her eyes, and played.

He recognized the song within the first few bars, and it both impressed and surprised him. He should stop her. It was a difficult and complex piece, even for the most accomplished violinist, and he didn't want to listen while she fucked up her chance at his scholarship. Yet, he couldn't because that moment in time served one purpose - for Celeste Walsh to play her violin for him.

Not that he thought for a second he might stop her. He couldn't. Not with the way she played. With Celeste, playing violin involved her entire body. She swayed at times. Others, she held still. No matter what, though, her face was a myriad of expressions while she held the bow and touched the strings as she would a lover.

She kept her eyes closed the entire time, and Lance felt as if he were peeking at a private or intimate moment. Her performance was one of the most erotic things he'd ever witnessed. In fact, music had never aroused him the way it did when she played. Never had he been so thankful for a table. He'd hate for her, or anyone for that matter, to see the erection her playing caused.

He wondered if anyone else had offered her a scholarship and this audition was just for fun? Had such passion filled all of her pervious auditions? Was she always so euphoric while she played? It was borderline obscene, and he loved it. He wanted more of it.

He wanted her.

She held him captive until the last note sounded and even when its echo had disappeared from the room, she held still, not yet releasing him from her spell. Until she moved, he didn't breathe.

Finally, she opened one eye and then the other, looking around almost as if she'd forgotten where she was. That wasn't possible, though, was it? She looked toward where he sat, the room's lighting did not allow her to see him, and for a second looked as if he'd caught her doing something naughty.

Holy hell. Did she get turned on playing the violin? He didn't know, but damn it all to hell, he would find out.

She remained on stage, clearly expecting him to dismiss her. He didn't feel bad in the least keeping her waiting. Her feet shifted the slightest bit. The small movement was so far the only hint she wasn't near as calm as she portrayed.

He picked up a paper from the pile in front of him and made it a point not to look at her when he spoke. "You're twenty-five?"

"Yes, sir."

Her unexpected use of 'sir' sent a shock throughout his body. He opened his mouth to tell her she didn't have to call him 'sir' but shut it just as quickly because he'd have added "Yet."

He kept his gaze even and uninterested when he lifted his head. "You're significantly older than most of your peers auditioning today."

She remained silent, and he nodded in approval. Yes, she would be a fun one. "Why are you only now applying to Juilliard?" he asked.

"After I graduated from high school, my grandmother came to live with us. My mom couldn't both watch her and do what she had been doing with the family business. I took over my Mom's role so she could care for her mother."

"What was your mother's job?"

"She was the pastry chef at our family's restaurant."

Impressive and not listed on her application. "You worked as a pastry chef for seven years?"

"I wasn't always the pastry chef. Sometimes I waited tables and sometimes I washed dishes."

He nodded, not interested in the past, and definitely not interested in listening about her washing dishes. "Why the violin? Why now?"

She shifted her gaze to somewhere beyond him, and her eyes took on a faraway look. "Because it's my time now. My time to stand on my own and to make something of myself. Because I love the violin and nothing would make me happier than to play it every day. And because I don't want to work in a restaurant all my life."

And she shouldn't, he thought. Not with the way she'd just played that piece. Working in a restaurant would waste her talent, and he couldn't allow that to happen. Not when he had a way to ensure it wouldn't.

He stacked the pile of papers in front of him and tapped them on the table. What was the name of the woman working on stage who ushered the applicants on and off? She'd introduced herself when he'd first arrived, but he hadn't made note of it, deciding it was a detail Richard could worry with. Which did him no good since he gave the man the boot.

"Thank you, Ms. Walsh," he said to the waiting woman on stage and smiled inwardly at the curt nod she gave in response and how she turned to walk away as if he'd excused her. "I did not say I excused you."

She froze and turned. "But you said -"

"Do not make it a habit to repeat back to me what I said. I have no trouble remembering my words, especially if I spoke them mere seconds before. What I said was, 'Thank you, Ms. Walsh' which in no way sounds like, 'You are excused.' Now, move back to where you were."

While she took the few necessary steps to return to her initial spot in the middle of the stage, he addressed those still waiting and the woman whose name he couldn't remember. "That's all for this year. Thank you for coming. You're excused." Ignoring the muttered protests, he turned his attention back to Celeste. "See how that works? The 'you're excused' part?"

She gaped at him in shock though. Probably wasn't hearing anything at all. From the look on her face, everything he said went in one ear and straight out the other. He didn't say anything else to her. Best she learn from the start how he operated.

The woman with the name he couldn't remember stepped out the shadows and onto the stage. She held one hand like a shield over her eyes, probably trying to see him better. "Mr. Braxton?"

"Yes." He knew what she would say, and he didn't want to hear it. After gathering together the few things he'd brought in, he walked to the stage.

As expected, as soon as his foot hit the first step, she appeared before him, flustered and flipping through pages on a clipboard. "There are three more violinists waiting backstage, and we haven't even started the brass group and...." Her voice trailed off when she looked up and saw him shaking his head.

"No," he said.

"No?"

"There will be no more auditions for this year's scholarship." Having made his way up the stairs to the stage, he turned to Celeste. "Get your things together and come with me."

BIG SWINGING D
DON'T MISS ISAAC AND MAGGIE'S STORY

Big Swinging D: Term used for the baddest badass on Wall Street. That guy. The one other men want to be and that women just want.

Maggie Warren has always been unfocused. She hops from job to job, and relationship to relationship. Most of the time, she's not even looking where she's going. Which is exactly what happens when she runs into Isaac Gregory, trips over her feet, and dumps a year's worth of compost all over his hand-stitched suit and one-of-a-kind leather shoes.

Isaac's never met anyone like Maggie. She's nothing like the women he works with, or the submissives he typically dates. Sure, she's got a knockout body and a wit to match, but she's a free spirit and hopelessly scattered. He should not be attracted to her. But he is.

After hearing she's between jobs, he offers her his recently vacated Personal Assistant position. She readily agrees, but isn't sure why he'd hire her. He's her exact opposite: structured, organized, and controlled.

Boy, does he like control. And it intrigues her, especially when she discovers his private life.

Isaac's not surprised when Maggie grows more and more interested in both of the worlds she sees him in: the public boardroom badass and the private well-respected Dominant. He tells her if she's interested, he has a plan. A plan so hedonistic it could only be proposed by the man nicknamed the Big Swinging D.

But even Wall Street isn't prepared for the fallout when the king of control falls for the queen of chaos.

Chapter One

Usually when Isaac Gregory's control slipped at work, he'd step outside of his Manhattan office building, walk for a block or two, and return, refreshed, and back on top of his game. Today, though, he could walk to Brooklyn and it wouldn't help. Matter of fact, if he made it that far, he'd keep going.

He'd expected his first day in three years without Lillian Bancroft as his personal assistant to be tough. Likewise, he'd known she'd be impossible to replace. However, if he'd had any idea how the first half of today would go, he'd have called in sick.

Part of the blame was his. After all, Lillian had given her resignation six weeks ago, leaving him plenty of time to hire a replacement. But, in what he could now admit was a delusional case of wishful thinking, he kept waiting for her to take it back.

Which was why he was on the phone seventy-two hours ago, desperate to find a temp able to start today while Lillian packed up her desk. And, okay, telling the owner and manager of the temp agency, "I don't care, just send whoever," was not one of his best moves, even when he added in the fact that it was then he realized Lillian was really leaving.

His concession on that point, however, in no way excused the temp the agency sent over this morning. Just thinking about the mess waiting for him back at the office made his head hurt. In less than three hours, the temp had "assisted" him by deleting two files of documents he needed for a ten o'clock meeting. Files she shouldn't have had access to, much less been able to delete. Then, because she didn't want to get in trouble for the deletion, had tried to fix it, and somehow, in a move that stumped his entire IT team, ended up encrypting another.

By the time she tip-toed to his desk at nine forty-five and, with tears in her eyes, whispered she was sorry, but she forgot to tell him his ten o'clock meeting had been moved up to nine, he was done. A quick phone call, and five minutes later, security escorted her from the building.

Unfortunately, not before he overheard her bemoaning to a group of administrative staff she never even got to see if his dick was really big or if the nickname was a misnomer. Fortunately, the rest of the staff knew his feelings toward that nickname and remained quiet.

He glanced at his watch and turned to head back to the office. He had a lot to do and no assistant to help. But on the upside, he couldn't see how his day could get worse.

Maggie Warren was late. Which wasn't saying much, she was often late. But today, she was really, really late. She quickened her step, shifting the heavy load of compost while trying to look around the container to ensure her path was clear.

So far so good.

She hated being late.

She blamed the 'if only.'

If only her most favorite author ever, or one of them, hadn't released a book today. And if only she hadn't been browsing online and saw the email alerting her with a link to purchase. And if only she hadn't decided to buy it and read just one chapter.

Because who could stop at one chapter?

She knew she had to stop using 'if only' as an excuse to justify everything. But how could she when all the fun stuff was stuff she shouldn't be doing and the stuff she was supposed to be doing was boring as hell?

"Like taking compost to the collection site," she mumbled.

Not that taking the compost to the collection site was all that bad; it was what would happen after she dropped off the compost. Because that was when she had to look for a real job.

She didn't have to get a job, but after almost a year and a half of working here and there and filling in where necessary, she recognized she needed the stability. Plus, she longed to be in an office where she saw the same people day after day. To be around a group of people she could build relationships with. Maybe go out to lunch or something.

And one day when she was ready, like in five years, maybe she'd find a guy she wanted to have sex with.

God, she missed sex.

Now, however, was not the time to think about sex. Not when she was carrying a massive amount of compost. Sex and compost did not mix well. At least not in her world.

With each step she grew more and more aware of her hands getting slippery. Not to mention how the sun and heat worked together to make the compost smell even worse. She hadn't thought about how she'd desperately need a shower after carting compost. There was no way around it, job hunting would have to wait for another day.

Her favorite thrift shop was just ahead and while she wouldn't be able to go inside, the owner, Max, always had the most amazing window displays. She'd look at it closer on the way back home, for now she only wanted a peek.

Shifting the weight of the compost, she drew nearer to the window. Max must have gotten in the pieces from the estate sale he'd told her about last week. Once she dropped off the compost, she'd window shop a little and come back tomorrow.

That would be perfect. She'd stop by around noon and take Max to lunch. He had a habit of getting caught up in his work and forgetting to eat since his wife of fifty years died ten months ago.

She turned back around, making a note to call Max when she got back to her apartment.

"Mama, look!" a little boy who couldn't have been over five yelled and ran past her.

Maggie barely kept a grip on the compost, but she managed, and breathed a huge sigh of relief when it didn't tumble out of her arms.

What in the world had caused the little boy to run past her like that? She turned her head to see better, but no luck. Maybe if she moved over just a touch...

She hit something hard and unyielding. There would be no save this time. The container fell out of her arms. She watched in horror as it tipped over and the lid flew off. In a matter of seconds, compost covered the hard and unyielding thing, which she now saw was the most gorgeous man who ever walked on earth.

He just didn't smell all that great at the moment.

ABOUT THE AUTHOR

NEW YORK TIMES/USA TODAY BESTSELLING AUTHOR

Even though she graduated with a degree in science, Tara knew she'd never be happy doing anything other than writing. Specifically, writing love stories.

She started with a racy BDSM story and found she was not quite prepared for the unforeseen impact it would have. Nonetheless, she continued and The Submissive Series novels would go on to be both New York Times and USA Today Bestsellers. One of those, THE MASTER, was a 2017 RITA finalist for Best Erotic Romance. Over one million copies of her books have been sold worldwide.

Visit her online at www.tarasueme.com

ALSO BY TARA SUE ME

THE SUBMISSIVE SERIES:

The Submissive

The Dominant

The Training

The Chalet*

Seduced by Fire

The Enticement

The Collar

The Exhibitionist

The Master

The Exposure

The Claiming*

The Flirtation

Mentor's Match

The Mentor & The Master*

Top Trouble

Nathaniel's Gift*

RACK ACADEMY SERIES:

Master Professor

Headmaster

BACHELOR INTERNATIONAL:

Mister Temptation (Previously American Asshole)

Mister Irresistible (Coming Soon)

Mister Impossible (Coming Soon)

THE DATE DUO:

The Date Dare

The Date Deal

WALL STREET ROYALS:

FOK

Big Swinging D

All or None

OTHERS:

Madame President

Bucked

Her Last Hello

Altered Allies (currently unavailable)

*eNovella

Made in the USA
Middletown, DE
20 July 2021